28 SECONDS

A HOUSE OF VALENTINE NOVELLA

Elizabeth Blair

VPK PUBLISHING

LITTLE ROCK ✧ DALLAS

Publisher's Note: This is a work of fiction. Names, characters, places and incidents are a product of the author's imagination. Locales and public names are sometimes used for atmospheric purposes. Any resemblance to actual people, living or dead, or to businesses, companies, events, institutions, or locales is completely coincidental.

Ordering Information:
Quantity sales. Special discounts are available on quantity purchases by corporations, associations, and others. For details, visit www.elizabethblairbooks.com.

28 Seconds / Elizabeth Blair – 2nd ed.
ISBN 13: 978-0692746356
ISBN 10: 0692746358
ASIN B01HN91TT6

CHAPTER ONE

Ariana, do something about your damn phone!"

The hard case bit into my kidneys, and I tried to inch away from the noise and responsibility it represented. It would be my mother. It was *always* my mother.

"Ariana!" Another voice from in the huddle of bodies groaned in annoyance.

"Working on it," I promised. I rolled over, feeling around in the sand for wherever my phone had landed. I clicked the button, blinking back from the brightness, and tried to focus on the screen. 34 messages. Wait...what? I struggled to sit, rubbing my face to clear the alcohol and sand that had to be fogging my vision.

"It's probably about last night."

I took a sideways glance at Donovan, a tourist who had served as my make-out partner for the evening before. "The bonfire's an annual thing. It's not news."

His hand traced up my bare leg, and he gave me a throaty laugh. "Maybe not but that video was pretty spectacular."

Last night that laugh had pulled me in made me reckless. In the pre-dawn light, it turned my stomach.

"What video?" I asked, my voice a slow growl.

Instead of answering, he pulled out his phone and pressed a few buttons then held the device out to me.

Bonfire flames flickering across the sand, the ocean black in the background.

Me doing a vodka induced dance number around the fire and chanting about the rum being gone.

28 seconds of embarrassing end of summer revelry.

"Did you post this somewhere?"

"Yeah, everywhere. It had like a thousand views even before we crashed. Pretty awesome, huh?"

I hit the play button again in sheer disbelief. 28 seconds of me in a bikini top and jean shorts. 28 seconds of the birthmark on my shoulder reflecting in the firelight. 28 seconds of me. Online. Viral. For anyone to see.

"Oh. My. God."

I wrestled out of his grasp, struggling to my feet as my head began to swim with the leftover alcohol. I grabbed the nearest dock pillar, holding tight and waiting for my balance to come back.

"Ariana?" He was up and beside me before I could breathe.

"He didn't know."

Someone, a supposed friend, was defending him from somewhere in the shadows. My fury rose, and I shoved Donovan back to the ground.

"Fucking tourists."

I ran like a crazy woman, tripping and tumbling across the sand as it sank beneath my feet. I zigzagged to the boardwalk as soon as possible but knew I had already lost precious time. I kicked my heels up, wishing I was more of an athlete than a bookworm. I clipped the corner to our house, barreled up the two tiny cottage stairs, and threw open the doors. "Mom!"

I rushed to the bottom floor, finding no one, and my heart leaped into my throat. I stood still, gasping for breath, and then heard the banging upstairs. I rushed up, skittering to a stop at my door when I saw her.

"It was a mistake, I swear! There was this tourist-" Her blinding look of terror silenced me.

"Help me," she ordered, yanking clothes out of my drawers and shoveling them into a duffel. "Now, Ariana, now!"

I didn't understand why or from who, but I was smart enough to know we were running. We had been running since I was five and this time was no different...except, for once, I knew it was all my fault. I grabbed my mother's hands, stopping her. "I'll get my stuff, go get yours."

Fear paralyzed her, and her eyes darted from the clothes to the door to me. "Five minutes. No more."

"Mom, I've got this." I gave her a quick hug to reassure her then pushed her toward the door. "Five minutes."

I zipped up the bag, not caring what was inside and took a last glance around the room. It still looked like a kid's room even though I'd graduated high school almost four years earlier: music band posters from my brief rocker phase; book quotes from my intellectual phase; instant photos of the friends I'd borrowed in the months we'd managed to stay here. I grabbed a handful of sea glass and tucked it into my pocket...the ocean was the only thing I'd miss anyway.

I stilled something suddenly out of sync. I did a slow pivot toward the hallway. It was nothing more than a creak of the stairs, a shadow along the wall, but the cold stillness of the once lively place was enough to make me scream. The shadows blurred into a blob, the sounds on the stairway now loud enough to wake the dead...my scream meant they no longer cared about being quiet.

"Get down!"

I don't know why I obeyed the command, but I did. I dropped to the floor, the splintered hardwood biting hard into my bare knees, just as something broke through the second-floor glass. A flash of movement caused me to lift my face. Strong fingers tightened around my throat, launching me backward and pinning me against the wall.

I hung there, in some weird mental suspension of my own making, while I tried to process the things that were happening. I was losing consciousness, I knew, but the trio of men behind my attacker caught my focus. They were strangers but calmer and more confident than the man holding me. Police, I thought, but then somehow knew better: they were too handsome, too strong, too cavalier and enjoyed themselves way too fucking much to be heroes.

Tiny little sparks broke into my vision, and I knew I was seconds from blacking out. Somewhere, my mother was in danger, and I was the only person who could help her. That's what we did- save each other. I twisted in his hands, trying for his groin but failing. I thrashed wildly and then did the only thing I could think of...I bit the hell out of him.

His grip loosened but didn't break and, just as I had resigned myself to never seeing my mother again, I saw the glint of metal at his waist. I wrenched it free, sticking it under his chin and firing before he could try and get it away. The shot ripped through his skull, splattering blood all over me as we both dropped to the floor.

"She's a little firecracker, isn't she?"

An arm was around my waist, pulling me back to standing. Strong... protective ...reassuring.

"*That* was our job." His breath was warm on my neck, his fingers brushing aside my wavy mass of beach blown hair to expose my shoulder. A grazing touch traced the scar on my flesh. When he spoke, his voice was both a threat and caress that sent shivers up my spine. "Ariana Valentine."

"No, you have the wrong person-"

"You," he chuckled, "have no idea who you are, and I don't have time to argue." He turned to the group of men beside him. "Find Teresa."

Teresa. My mom. My best friend.

"No!"

His arms locked around me, holding me in place. I twisted, kicking and thrashing, but he only tightened his grip. The cold metal of his gun pressed against my back, searing into my skin, and angry, hysterical tears began to stream down my face.

I lifted my eyes and saw him step into the room: shorter than the others with sandy hair that made him an oddity in their dark brood; rough hands, calloused and weathered; devilish green eyes that were watching me with smug satisfaction. I stopped moving, breathing, unable to process the terror that enrobed me.

"Breathe, Ariana."

I gulped for air, but it didn't help. Visions of what they might do to my mother mixed with flashes of violent action movies and I felt the vodka from last night rising. "I'm gonna be sick."

He released me, and I dropped to my knees, spewing the contents of my stomach at his feet. He knelt beside me, his hand on my head. "Better?"

I skittered away from him just as my mother rushed into the room, sliding across the floor to pull me into her arms. His gun was already out, pointing somewhere over my head and I twisted her around to be between them.

"Mom-"

"Cole, Ariana. Trust only Cole. Promise me."

"I don't know a Col-"

But someone was trying to wrench her away and her words cut off. One gunshot. The two staccato ones right after. A barrage of fire, muffled by the walls, reverberating from somewhere in the tiny house. And then silence.

A hand reached around me, touching my mother's throat but I batted it away. She was dead. I knew it without needing to check. She was half of me, clearly the better half. It had been the two of us against the world, and now I was alone.

"We're clear."

The monster hovering over me gave some nonverbal response that caused the other men to step into the room.

"Sedate her and then we'll get her in the car."

"Yes, sir."

I rocked my mom, divided between wanting to bring her back and wanting to join her in whatever peaceful place she'd escaped to. A tiny prick drew my attention back to the room, and I managed a few curse words.

"Yep, she's a spitfire alright."

A soft, warm chuckle. "She always was. Torch this place. I want nothing but rubble."

"Cole, you want-"

"Just do it," he ordered, and a rush of air signaled their departure.

"Cole," I murmured. I could feel my body loosening, my arms growing heavy. My hands weakened, and I could feel her slipping from my grasp. Strong hands reached to take her, resting her body gently back on the carpet. "Cole."

His fingers were light on my chin, tipping my head towards him. His other hand reached to my wrist, two fingers pressing into my veins as he counted in a soft hum. "Look at me, Ariana."

I nodded, obeying. "You have brown eyes."

"So do you."

"You smell like balsam and seawater."

My brain fogged, and his laugh came out as a tinkling chime. "You smell like blood and vomit."

"That's...unattractive," I said, struggling for the words.

"She's not out, yet?"

"Tolerance of a horse, this one," Cole grumbled. "Give her another shot."

"But-"

"Do it! We've got to get moving."

This time, I felt nothing but the warmth beginning to spread quicker. I fell back against his chest, and my head bounced once as if I'd hit stone. He barked more orders I couldn't understand and then his fingers were on my wrist again. "Ariana-"

"Look at you, I know." I managed to lift my head, but my vision wouldn't focus. "I'm trying."

"You're doing fine. Can you tell me what happened?"

I screwed my face up. "Something bad. Something very bad."

"Yes."

"My mom," I whispered. "She's gone."

"Yes."

"And I killed someone."

He chuckled. "Executed more like but, yes, yes you did."

"But I'm still here. I don't want to be here still."

"Then we'll go. Are you ready to go?"

"Yes." I tried to stand, even thought I was standing, but then realized I hadn't moved. "No. You're going to kill me."

"I'm not going to kill you," he promised. "But we really, really do have to go."

"Okay. I'll trust you."

"That," he grunted as he lifted me up and tucked me into his arms, "is something we'll discuss once you're sober."

CHAPTER TWO

The first time I awoke, everything was a confusing mix of sounds and smells. Male voices arguing mixed with the honk and screech of traffic; an antiseptic scent like a hospital layering over rusty seawater and bitter coffee. My eyes scanned the room, taking in the bad art that denoted a hotel room before settling on an over-sized window. Tiny slivers of light slipped through, forming shadows, and it took several minutes before my eyes adjusted to see the two men talking in hushed tones.

Cole. He was okay because my mom had said so. He was watching me, knew I was awake, but made no move to come forward. And then the sandy-haired man from the house. A feeling or memory started to bubble up at the sight of him, and my body began to shake. Cole's eyes shot from me to him just seconds before I started screaming. Another pinprick and then blackness.

The second time I was more coherent. My eyes flashed to where I expected the men to be, but only Cole remained. He was sitting at a small table, a cheap lamp made to look expensive casting a yellow glow over a stack of papers. I rolled in the bed, checking the opposite side of the room.

"He's not here." Cole's calming voice was beside me.

"Who?"

"Marco. Considering how you screamed at the sight of him, I thought it best to send him next door." He touched my elbow, and I extended my arm in a familiar dance as he checked my pulse. "No more screaming, okay? It's getting hard to explain to the hotel staff."

I nodded.

"Obedience is a good trait to have in the Valentine family. It will serve you well." He let my arm go and then tucked the covers back around me. "Why does he scare you?"

I felt the fear rise again but shook my head. "I don't know. Where are we?"

"Boardwalk, Atlantic City." I struggled to sit, but his soft push held me down. "Give yourself a few more minutes. I'll have someone come in and help you get a shower."

"What are you giving me?"

"A cocktail of designer drugs. Nothing long term or addictive, I assure you. A Valentine exclusive some would say."

"Rohypnol," I murmured, "and ecstasy? Mixed with something else. I'm not sure."

His arms dropped around me, caging me and forcing me to look at him. "How would you know that?"

My fingers traced the chiseled line of his jaw, hearing the rough scratch of his stubble against my palm. His intensity was breathtaking. "Modafinil?"

I could hear his teeth clench, feel the twitch in his jaw. "Yes."

"Cole, my mother-"

"She's dead, Ariana."

"I know that," I managed. "I was coated in her blood for chrissakes."

"How " he hissed, "can you remember that?"

The grimace on his face wasn't attractive, and I tried to brush it away with the pads of my fingers. My tears welled but didn't fall, and I locked my eyes with his. "How could I possibly not?"

My response was clearly not the right one, and his body tensed, the stress etching across each muscle. I lowered my voice to a whisper, a soft plea meant only for his ears. "Cole, can you make me not remember? Please?"

"I'm trying, Ariana," he grumbled. "I'm fucking trying."

Failure. He was failing at his task, and it made him angry. I didn't want him angry. "Can I get a shower now? You can try and figure out why your cocktail isn't any better than tequila."

"On you."

"What?"

"It's not working on you," he explained. "Half a dose will take down any person on the planet. Except you."

I struggled to get up again and this time, he allowed me to move. "Shower. And maybe a bottle of tequila. Let's start there."

He nodded and moved to the door, opening it a sliver to bark some orders. In seconds, a woman decades older than my mother stepped in. He talked to her in a hushed voice, exchanging news I assumed, and then she came for me.

"Help her get cleaned up," he ordered, "and then up her dosage."

"She's already getting-"

"I don't care. Do it."

The last time I awoke, I could almost believe nothing was real. There was no bad in my life much less the world. I knew I was in a strange hotel room somewhere near an ocean but not where I had been living. The smell was different, the temperature colder. I had only skinny dipped once in my life...with my mother, no less. It had been somewhere like this. Cold, with water more gray than blue.

I had turned fourteen and had just finished having my first period. My mother and her wild gypsy ways had decided we needed to celebrate and wanted to make me realize that it wouldn't always be about the pain. We stripped down, and she was in the water fast, but I was still too young to be embarrassed about my body. I stood on the beach, reveling in the way the sea spray assaulted every inch of my skin, even parts I couldn't touch myself. The smell of the water blocking out all memories, the wind caressing my flesh as if it were a lover I would one day meet.

My hand went to my skin, remembering the feel of it, remembering the taste of the salt on my lips. Somewhere in my brain, I knew I was naked in bed, and it was starched sheets brushing against me, but my mind fought harder telling me I was back on that beach. The confusion in my head caused a whimper to escape as I tried to make the euphoria of that beach mesh with the terror of where I now lay.

"Well, we know the ecstasy kicked in at least." Cole's voice echoed in my head from paces away. His low, throaty laugh was like a lifeline. I let the sound wash over me, remembering the razor-like feel of his body pressing into mine. The cold steel of his gun pressing into my back alternating with the heat of him when his arms had held me prisoner to keep me safe.

My brain told me to stop that there were more important things to think about, but my body refused to listen. My hand slipped over my breasts, down my stomach, and between my thighs. Wet, so desperately wet. Flashes of his body against mine, his breath hot on my throat, his touch silky on my wrist...I promised myself I would stop, would only allow myself a single stroke against my clit. But then it wasn't just imaginary, and his body was next to mine, his lips hot against my throat.

"Need any help with that?"

I bit my lip, confusion pouring from my being. I'd never done anything like this...allowing someone to witness this most private act. I barely knew him and my mother...my mother. Conflicting emotions raged, and I willed myself to behave, but my body had some mind of its own and, even as my internal protests fought, my fingers continued their fiery strokes. Desperation seized me, and I let out a broken gasp wanting it - the lust, the tears, the heartbreak, the memories - to all just end.

He wouldn't ask twice. I knew that a single word would get me what I needed. I just had to summon the courage to ask. "Cole, please."

His hand shoved mine aside, his palm rough against the slickness of my folds. My hips arched me into his palm, and he slid one finger inside me, then another. I spread wider, desperate for more as his fingers plunged deeper. I loved the sound of it...his hand slapping against my sex, the suction as he plunged in and out. My juices coated everything, my thighs, his hand, the clean sheets.

I never knew I could want, need, something so much. Why had I ever denied myself something that could feel like this?

"Christ, Ariana." His voice held the same incredulity I felt: how could anyone possibly be so wet?

A half dozen times I got so close but each time, dark thoughts shadowed everything, and I'd back inches away from the edge. My hands thrust to his hair, tightening into little fists and pulling his head closer to mine. His eyes were on me, dark and intense, as my tears of frustration and grief started to fall.

As if he knew my thoughts, his lips moved to my ear, his voice calm but tinged with a ragged desire of his own. "Baby girl," he ordered, "for chrissakes, drop the guilt and just let it come."

And I did. His fingers slipped in again, slow and deep, as his thumb circled hard against my clit. Two tiny circles and I buried my teeth into his shoulder to keep from screaming. My body shuddered with the release, but he held firm, never wavering. I had never felt something so complete, so utterly engulfing, that it made my every thought, my every memory, disappear. My breathing took minutes to calm, my body even longer to settle and yet he never moved. When I took a final shuddering breath, I let my eyes drift to his, fighting down the embarrassment I felt building as the last echoes of the drug burned off.

"You," he whispered, "are dangerously intoxicating."

I had no idea the proper response for that so I traced the half-moons on his shoulder instead. "I made you bleed."

"I didn't even notice," he assured me. "Never again, let the darkness of this world keep you from living, understood?"

His voice was still rough and jagged, and I let myself look at him, actually look at him, for the first time. The darkest of brown eyes, olive skin, peppered with a stubble along his rugged jawline, a chest twice as wide as my body, all rigid muscle. Strength. Power. Safety. And a desire still smoldering just beneath it all. My hand snaked from his shoulders and traced a slow path down to his pants, a stone hard bulge threatening to come unleashed. I grazed his cock, just barely, and his hand grabbed mine, locking it against the bed.

"No."

"But-"

"Consider this a one-time gift." His eyes did a slow, sensuous exploration down my body and I could feel a warm tug growing again in my lower abdomen. He must have seen or felt my need rising again because he moved a pace away, standing up and adjusting himself to be less obvious. "Welcome back to the house of Valentine, Ariana. I'll go get you that tequila."

CHAPTER THREE

N o sleeping yet." Cole shook my hip and waved a cup of coffee under my nose.

"That is *not* tequila," I grunted, rolling away from him.

Cold hard glass touched my back, and he waved the bottle in his other hand back and forth. "Coffee first, tequila after."

"After what?"

"I have questions. You have questions. Let's see if we can get some of them answered." He moved to the little table and sank into a chair, sipping his own cup. "Bridgett put some clothes for you in the bathroom. I think you may have missed them earlier."

Tugging the sheet around me, I yanked it out of the mattress and headed to get dressed.

"Now you're shy?" he chuckled, and I could feel the blush rising over my entire body. I was back, moments later, in respectable jeans and a tee-shirt, both in brands too expensive for me to have even heard of much less own. I dropped into the chair opposite him, curled my knees into my chest, and then cupped the steaming mug in my hands. I took a tiny sip and closed my eyes. "Bitter. Excellent."

"Before we get to business, do we need to talk about-" his hand waved toward the bed.

I shook my head, the blush still close to the surface. "No. Absolutely not."

He smiled, a sexy, self-assured grin that made my eyes drop away. He tapped a few of the papers on the table. "Okay then. You and your mother have been going by Ariana and Teresa Serrano for how long?"

"That's our name."

"Humor me."

"Since I was five and first registered for school. That's as far back as I remember."

"You remember nothing-"

"My turn," I said, cutting him off. "What's *your* name?"

"You are an afterthought kind of girl, aren't you? Be scared later, be shy later, ask names later," he laughed. "Cole Serrano."

A vision of his fingers deep inside me caused my eyes to flash to the bed and then back to him.

He grinned, knowing my thoughts. "No relation, I assure you. It seems your mother stole my surname when she fled with you. Genius, really. You would think she would choose something like Smith or Williams, but while everyone was searching for the common, she defied logic. No one ever thought to look for a Valentine or a Serrano. Risky, but damn genius."

I swelled with pride. Whatever we were running from, she had obviously earned his respect in doing it.

"You remember nothing before then? Really?"

I paused, thinking. "I get snippets sometimes. Things I don't remember, but I can see them like a movie reel. When I was little, my mom told me they were from an action movie I'd just forgotten I'd seen."

"So they're violent?"

"Yes."

He waited for further explanation, but I gave him nothing. "But you didn't believe her completely; I take it? That's why you were willing to keep running. Is Marco one of those?"

"Who?"

"No games, Ariana."

I sighed. "Maybe. I don't know. It's more a feeling than a memory. He just...I don't want him near me."

"Then that will be arranged." His touch was light on my knee. "If you remember, though, I need to know. Immediately. Agreed?"

I nodded. "When you came in the house you checked my birthmark."

"It's a scar, not a birthmark."

"No, my mom-"

"Told you many things to keep you safe. Not all were true."

He stretched out his arm and tugged up the edge of his sleeve. A white scar gleamed against his olive skin, buried in the flesh of his wrist. I sat my mug down, taking his hand in mine, and traced the rough mark with trembling fingers. Smaller than mine, only the size of a quarter, and yet almost identical in every other way. He pulled away and refilled my coffee before settling back in his chair.

"It's a brand. It shows allegiance to the house of Valentine."

"A brand? As in, burning into flesh? Tell me you are joking."

"Afraid not. Your mother had one as well. At the nape of her neck." He motioned to his own neck where it would be, and then his voice lowered. "Why don't you ask me the question you really want to know?"

Fear and frustration washed over me, and I untucked my legs to move. Before my feet touched the floor, he had me locked back in the chair, power radiating off him. "No more running, Ariana."

"Why are we running?"

He sat back, a quizzical look on his face. "That's what you want to know most? Not about the Valentine family, your family?"

I bristled. "I'm not an idiot. A group of men sweeps in with lots of guns, manages to burn a house down with no worries of police interference, has a limitless supply of drugs, and then whisks me away to Atlantic City with no questions asked? The Valentine crime family makes the news even in small towns, Cole, so don't patronize me."

His hand went to his face, raking the stubble on his jawline. His eyes darkened, and I could only imagine the thoughts and conclusions he was trying to draw in his head.

I couldn't help the sarcastic bite to my words. "Does my intelligence shock you?"

"No," he murmured, "not at all. Your mother was the most brilliant person I've ever known. What I don't understand is why you remember any of that. You shouldn't have anything except maybe foggy visions of déjà vu."

"You keep saying that," I grumbled.

"Half a dose knocks grown men to their knees. They're out for three to four days, and when they wake, they recall nothing. Not a single memory of the days they've lost."

"So?"

"Ariana, you've had six full doses in less than 48 hours, and you remember *everything*."

I was quiet, considering. I wasn't exactly innocent where drugs or alcohol were concerned. Small towns didn't have much entertainment and getting stoned or drunk was the limit of weekend options. My mother was the free spirited sort and, as long as she knew I was safe, was content to let me experiment and find my own way. But I'd never gone too far into that world...it was a temporary diversion but never some great addiction that would have provided me a herculean tolerance level.

"How did you know what was in the mix? You guessed perfectly, and only a handful of people know that recipe. It's like the family's trademark and is an extraordinarily well-guarded secret."

"Well guarded meaning they kill for it. Yeah, I get it." I shook my head, tired of being talked to like a child. "I don't know. My mom worked in a pharmacy, and we talked about drugs all the time. Legal and illegal...it was just general conversation over the years."

"That wouldn't-"

"Cole, I said I don't know!" I could see him retreating, and I exhaled a long breath. "Sorry."

"You've been through hell, Ariana. Don't apologize when I'm the one being an ass." He offered me a half smile. "You still love the ocean, right? I found the sea glass in your shorts."

I nodded, still stubbornly avoiding him.

"Grab the shot glasses and let's take this tequila to the beach. Get out of this place for a while." He extended his hand, and I took it without thinking. Once I was on my feet, though, I hesitated. He tucked the glasses into my hands and pulled me behind him. "It's safe. I promise."

CHAPTER FOUR

We walked in silence, a half mile down the beach to where it was empty. Darkness was starting to fall, and I realized I didn't even know what day it was. Nor did I really care. "You're sure it's safe?"

"Yes. There's not even teenage morons wielding video cameras."

"Ugg." I dropped into the sand, and he followed suit, cracking open the tequila. "Tell me the Valentine family power made that disappear."

He laughed. "Yes, it did."

I drew circles in the sand. "It's my fault, you know. If it hadn't been for that video-"

"Hey." His touch was light on my leg. "Don't do that to yourself. You would have been found eventually. The internet has made the world a much smaller place. Teresa recognized that, prepared for that. So do *not* blame yourself."

I nodded but didn't respond. Instead, I inhaled deep, letting the scent and sound of the surf calm my senses.

"You know, you are technically not old enough to even have this," he said, slipping a glass into my hand.

"Says the drug kingpin that sells his wares to school children?"

"Not my customer base. I do have some ethics," he grunted then touched his glass to mine. "But touché."

We downed the shots in unison, and he was already pouring more as the numbing sting slid down my throat. "God, that was stupid. He was, like, sixteen, and such a dumbass."

"Like them young, do you?"

The tequila steeled my nerves, and I smiled at him. "Depends. How old are you?"

"A decade older than your kid and probably ten decades smarter."

I smiled to myself...twenty-six. Still in my eligibility range then. Not that it had mattered earlier. I hadn't even cared about his name. "I was in a string bikini right next to him, and he was more excited that people liked his fucking video. I wanted to strangle him."

"Did you?" He laughed at the glare I sent him. "You *are* a Valentine, Ariana. It's a fair question."

"No, but I shoved him on his ass."

"Good for you."

I swallowed my own shot and then his. "So what does that mean exactly? My mother had an affair with some mafia henchman? I know she had me when was crazy young."

"Fifteen," he admitted. "But no, nothing so simple as that. The mafia isn't involved in the drug trade. Legal or illegal, the drug trade is our sole source of income. Ariana, your father, is Franco Valentine."

I shrugged. The name meant nothing to me, and I waited for him to explain the significance.

"He's head of the family."

"Your boss."

"My employer," he corrected.

"So saving me was simply doing his bidding?" It didn't hurt as much as I thought to say the words out loud. Thank God for tequila.

"No. I work for him, and my allegiance is to the Valentine family. But my loyalty," he paused to take another shot, "was and always has been to your mother."

"You know I don't understand that."

"It's a complicated tree. I'll draw you a chart one day."

"Soon."

"Soon," he acknowledged.

I stretched out in the sand, making half sand angels. "Nothing smells like a boardwalk. The salt, the grease, the sugary taffy, the leftover trash and seagull shit."

"You told me I smell like seawater."

"Did I? I don't remember."

"I think we've established *that's* a lie."

"And the sound. Happy kids, crying kids, stressed parents, and lovers with gunshots and sirens mixed in. It's like the freedom of childhood with the awful reality of life thrown into a frozen margarita machine and blended until there's no way to tell the difference."

"Philosophy major?" he guessed.

"Not hardly. I'm a science nerd."

"What branch?"

I grimaced. "Stupid Valentine genes."

"Let me guess...biochem?" I gave him a scathing glare in response, and his body rocked with laughter. He tried to speak but was laughing so hard it came out in broken gasps. "Oh my god, Ariana, that is fucking priceless."

"Fuck you, Cole."

His laugh was so earnest, so free, that I couldn't help but smile at him. He pushed another drink my direction as a peace offering, and I sat up just enough to down it before dropping down again. He took his own then stretched out his legs alongside me as he tried to calm his laughter. "Fucking priceless. You want another?"

"I'm good. This is a happy place."

He took one of his own before capping the bottle. "You were raised here, you know."

"The beach? That would make sense then."

"No. This beach. This Boardwalk. Atlantic City. You were born here."

I twisted to use his legs as a pillow, playing with the bottle he'd stuck in the sand. "Were it not for the tequila, I would be furious that you know so much about a life I can only imagine."

"What else does the tequila tell you?"

"Nothing. And that's what makes it so damn wonderful, and so much better than your useless drug."

His touch was light on my head, brushing back loose tendrils of hair. "Are you forgetting?"

I shook my head. "But I'm going numb to everything and right now, that's just as good."

"Everything?" A single finger stroked down my throat, sending visible shivers down my body. He was grinning at me, and I swatted his hand away.

"Okay, maybe not everything. But since you said that's not an option-"

"Blame the tequila for my transgressions."

I laughed. "Damned tequila."

His hand was soft against my face, tracing around my eyes and down to my lips. "Your laugh is the most beautiful sound in the world."

"I don't do it often," I admitted.

"I figured, and that," he murmured, "is what makes hearing it so beautiful. The way you've handled everything, the way you've pulled yourself together is the most remarkable thing I've ever seen."

"I wasn't given much of a choice, was I?"

"No," he murmured, "I suppose not."

"Cole, did I really kill him?" I asked, my words a broken whisper.

"Yes. I'm sorry I can't take away that memory for you."

I was silent a few minutes, listening to the waves and trying to block out all thought. "Cole?"

"Hm?"

"Will you tell me about my mom? Happy things."

He smiled and kissed the palm of my hand before pressing it back to my stomach and interlacing our fingers. "Teresa was a force like none other. Full of life and a rebellious little gypsy. Always a handful, your dad called her. God, did he love her. Would've given her the world...tried to, in fact."

"He loved her?" I frowned. That made no sense. Why would she run from someone who loved her so completely?

"He's never loved anyone else, Ariana. Your mother...she raised me, you know. Teresa was the only parental figure I ever knew. Until she left with you, my world revolved around the two of you."

"But she left you behind?"

He gave me a patient look that was almost infuriating. "I helped her get away."

I closed my eyes, trying to remember anything he was telling me. But no matter how hard I tried to paint the pictures of the scenes he was giving me, nothing would surface. And then I saw it: a man's hand curling across a dress with tiny pink flowers, a woman's hand knocking it away and shouting. So very much shouting. And pain...like little shocks of lightning coursing through my body. I jerked up from the sand, weaving from the tequila, but Cole was beside me fast, his strong arms encircling my waist to keep me from falling.

"What was that?"

I broke free from his touch, taking several steps away. "Nothing. Too much tequila."

"That was *not* tequila."

"Cole!" We both jerked at the shout, turning to face the group of men headed our way. "Company's coming. Half an hour maybe."

He nodded, nonplussed. "We'll move to the house. Get everything from the hotel."

"The house isn't ready-"

"Make it ready. Any news on Franco?"

"No change."

"We're running?" My hands wrapped around my stomach, hugging myself. "Again?"

"No. Just moving a few blocks," Cole assured me. "We were having your house cleaned. Unlike the hotel, it's a fortress."

"My house?" I frowned but backed away when he started for me. He hesitated at my skittish behavior, and it was just long enough for Marco to appear in front of me. His fingers buried in my arms, yanking them apart and pulling me toward him.

"We'll get her over there."

"Move away from her."

"What?" Confusion etched across his face, but I didn't care how irrational it seemed. From somewhere within, I launched a full assault on him: kicking, thrashing, punching. But it only caused his grip to tighten, and I could feel the anger begin to consume him. He shook me violently, my head snapping back and forth.

Cole, calm with no hint of drunkenness, was beside us. He murmured a few words, but Marco was beyond hearing, his rage unquenchable...until Cole raised a gun inches from his face.

The moving stopped, but Marco's hands tightened with such incredible force that I couldn't reign in a pain filled scream before it escaped. The other men circled us, enclosing us, but I had no idea which side they were even on. Cole leaned forward, touching the muzzle to Marco's temple.

"Get that damn thing away from me," he hissed. "I've served this family since before you were even fucking born."

"Then you should know that I will send a bullet through your skull without a moment's regret if you don't: *Let. Her. Go.*"

I could feel his hands twitching, and I could tell he was considering ignoring Cole's demand. He smiled at me, dark and menacing and then let me go with a firm jerk. He sneered, his voice a taunt that cut into my soul: "Welcome back, littlest Valentine."

CHAPTER FIVE

"The men say you haven't left this room in over an hour. Not up to exploring just yet?"

I grimaced at the knowledge he was keeping such close tabs on me. I hadn't, in fact, bothered to explore this house that was now apparently mine. From gossip between the black suited men, I'd learned that this was the house where I grew up. With a dozen or so bedrooms, a library, and chef-worthy kitchen, I hadn't had the energy even to try and check out the place. Instead, I'd found a back den on the lower level that had huge old fashioned hand crank windows that overlooked the ocean beach across the road and decided this was far enough into their world.

Cole stepped behind from somewhere in the darkness, his hand resting on my hip. His other slipped down one arm, two fingers resting on my wrist. I tilted my head to him without being asked and mumbled, "look at me, Ariana."

He chuckled but didn't stop counting. Whatever the result was, it didn't make him happy. He tugged on my waist. "Come, lay down for a bit."

"You can't seem to stop touching me."

"I admit you are curiously inviting."

Rather than move, I interlinked our fingers and snaked his hand beneath the fabric of my shirt to lay against my skin. I couldn't blame my actions on the drugs or alcohol this time: it was the memories of my mother; the fast escape; the new found family; the drugs; and the terrifying visions, that were driving my sudden desperate need for this man to be touching me.

"You're trembling."

"It's just the adrenaline."

"Like it was just the tequila?"

He stepped away, leaving me feeling empty and alone. I wrapped my arms around myself to stave off the shaking, but it only seemed to make it worse. He was giving soft commands at the door and then, thankfully, returned to stand behind me. His hands slipped back under my shirt, interlinking at my navel.

"You still don't remember Marco?"

I shook my head. "I don't think I want to either."

"He certainly knows you. I've sent him away."

"Because that worked so well last time?" I mumbled and could feel him tense.

"I *am* sorry about that. I underestimated the situation. It won't happen again. I've sent him on assignment out of state."

"I didn't know; so how could you have possibly known?" I said, squeezing his hand. "I'm just still trying to shake it off. I didn't mean to attack you."

"You didn't attack me, Ariana. You told the truth. I'm just pissed at myself for it," he grumbled.

"What did he mean 'littlest Valentine'?"

"You are the youngest, I suppose."

A knock interrupted us, but Cole made no attempt to move. He called over his shoulder, directing them to put the trays down on the table. "Food," he explained. "You still haven't eaten. Will you try and eat something?"

His concern made me smile. It was something my mother would have done...although the warmth and comfort I felt in his arms was anything but motherly.

"Is this concern for my well-being or you trying to get in my pants?"

"Both," he winked, "always both."

I moved to sit on the sofa, checking over the choices. Light things - fruit, cheese, crackers - appetizer fair. It all made my stomach wrench. I grabbed a slice of apple to nibble just to keep him from glowering at me. "I don't have siblings, right? So it's a weird phrase."

"True. Why do you ask?"

"It felt..." I trailed off, uncertain.

"Threatening?"

"No... dirty."

"Dirty?" Cole sank into the chair beside me. "Ariana-"

"Sorry, that sounded inane, didn't it?"

"No." He shook his head, his eyes flashing. "It sounded really fucking disturbing."

"So what were you whispering about with those men when we got back to the house?"

"That was a pathetic attempt to deflect."

"Agreed, but you are going to let me get away with it because you have something more important to talk to me about."

"First, I'd let you get away with almost anything. Second, it's unnerving that you somehow know I have another topic to discuss. And third-"

"You are afraid that Marco just became more important than you ever considered." I tapped my head. "Observant. Is that a Valentine trait? Because my mother was totally *not* observant."

"Yes, it is. Nothing gets by your father. *Ever.* Are you going to eat that or simply chew on it until I leave?"

"Neither," I grumbled and tossed it back on the tray. "So what do you need to tell me?"

He settled back in the chair. "As a biochem major, you know about Valentine Pharmaceuticals. I'll guess you also know the rumors about the darker side of the company as well."

"I think we've established the rumors to be true."

"Not where I was headed with this conversation but yes, I suppose we have confirmed that for you as well."

"So where are we headed with this conversation?"

"Tony, the big guy? He's a former marine. He was stationed overseas during the Gulf War, serving more tours than any man should and his demons followed him home. He became addicted to a wide variety of substances. Except for alcohol. No idea why that escaped his resume."

"Even the president drinks. Alcohol allows the illusion of control and stability...two things no true addict cares about."

"That is an excellent theory. Brilliant actually." He frowned as if it hadn't occurred to him. "Whatever the case, he's clean now and one of our top employees."

"Yes, I noticed you keep him close. I'm still not following."

"His specialty, so to speak, is drug interactions. How they combine and cause either positive or negative affect to the user and... I'd like him to take a look at you."

"Pardon?"

"Your reaction isn't normal. It's possible you had something in your system already-"

"Yeah, a fifth of vodka."

"I timed your last dose of Valentine to the second. Your heart rate is still spiking, you've had no appetite for anything but sex, coffee, and alcohol, and your flashbacks are increasingly more violent." He touched my knee. "Ariana, this is what we do. We've spent our lives in this business and your reaction is *not* normal."

Worried...he was worried. Not only that but there was an undercurrent of guilt that was easy to recognize. He was afraid that he'd done some lasting damage with the amount of drugs he'd pumped through my system. I exhaled, long and shuddering, to try and steel myself, and then started with the easiest first.

"Coffee equals my mother. After we moved or fled or whatever, on my very first day of school my mom told me that I was such a big girl that I could have coffee with her. Every day, no fail, she would wake me with a cup of fresh espresso and we would sit together. Sometimes we'd talk, sometimes it was complete silence.... but it was always the two of us and our mugs of coffee. It wasn't even *good* coffee but, it was her."

He pushed aside the trays of food, moving to sit on the coffee table across from me. "I'm sorry, Ariana, for your loss. I should have said that a long time ago."

I waved him off because I knew if he said more I would fall apart. "The alcohol makes me numb. Just like anyone, I suppose. It drowns away everything, so I can postpone facing anything. Cowardly, I know, but right now it's all I'm capable of."

"You are not a coward. A coward would not have taken a man's own gun and shot him point blank in the head. A coward would not have tried to fight off Marco Savatini with her bare fucking hands."

"Sex is, well sex," I offered, quick to change the subject. "It's a release; I'm young, and it's uncomplicated."

"No one on the planet would agree with that statement."

"Well, it *was* uncomplicated until you showed up in my bedroom."

"For the record, I have no intention of complicating your life any further."

"So you have made abundantly clear despite how very many times I find your hands on my body." He frowned, just as I knew he would. "Which leads us to my heart rate. You know my body's reaction to you because yours is the same. You are something real, your touch tethering me to the only thing I know to be true. Why would my heart rate *not* spike?"

It took a minute, but a slow smile spread across his face. "While I don't doubt your sincerity, I have a memory for you. When I was a kid, your dad gave me a super expensive bike that I'd begged for. It was perfect: cherry red, chrome, shiny tires - a kid's wet dream. I'd had it two days before I tried to launch it off Steel Pier. It went flying; it was this damn perfect arc...before it went crashing into the ocean. I survived, but that bike didn't have a chance. I was distraught. Not only had I lost the best gift ever, but I'd also destroyed what your father had entrusted me with. To my little kid brain, I'd just sunk the equivalent of a Bugatti Veyron into the Atlantic on a fucking whim.

You were four, and I came home to find you sitting on the porch of this very house. When I asked you how the hell I was supposed to face your dad because I knew, just knew he was going to kill me, you had the simplest of solutions: compliment him. You told me to compliment him, and he'd never realize there was a lie buried in the truth." He leaned forward, his hands clasping between his legs as he watched me. "I've no idea what part of your words was a lie, or what you think you need to hide from me, but you should be aware that while you can undoubtedly fool any person on the planet, you cannot fool me."

"What I said about you was true."

"But?"

I shifted off the sofa, walking back to the picture window. I tried to crank it open, but my hands were shaking too much even to get a grip on it. Cole was beside me, throwing them open in a split second. I inhaled the salty breeze, listening to the sound of the surf crashing in regular intervals, and ignoring Cole's desperate check of my blood pressure. It would be immeasurable, I knew.

"Fuck, Ariana." He tried again, assuming his count had been wrong. "I'm gonna get Tony. I'll be right back-"

"No," I held him back. "Just give me a minute. Please." I climbed onto the window seat, pressing my knees to my chest, and began counting the seconds between the waves. When I'd hit two hundred, I exhaled and offered my wrist up to Cole.

He counted. "Better," he admitted. "Still not good but better." He sat down beside me, lifting up my legs and crossing them over his. His voice was soft, a request rather than a command. "But?"

I dropped my head back against the wall, my eyes closing. Though I tried to concentrate on the ocean sounds, knowing it would settle me, it took only moments for the silent tears to start falling.

"I've been with the Valentine family for twenty-six years. The darkness, depravity, and betrayal that I've witnessed during that time is unfathomable. There is nothing you could tell me that would surprise me or make me walk away."

I hesitated a second longer than he was willing to wait. "Ariana, I cradled you and your mother in my arms as she died. I helped wipe her blood, and the blood of the man you killed, from your skin. I've had my hands on every part of your body. I've had them *inside* you for chrissakes. I've listened to you beg my name as you come. What could possibly be more private than any of those things?"

"The flashbacks were not brought on by the stress of my mother's death or by Valentine," I clipped before I lost my nerve.

"The flashbacks," he murmured with a half-smile. "You were distracting me so I wouldn't realize you failed to explain them. Clever, Ariana, very clever. Have you always had them then?"

I nodded.

"For how long?"

"When I was little, just in school, they were constant. Like every night. My mom said it was the stress of moving, and they did start going away. Never completely but down to once or twice a month maybe."

"And now how often?"

"Now?"

"Since your mother's death."

I shrugged, not trusting my voice.

"Ariana, how often?"

"Twice a day," I murmured, "sometimes more."

His head dropped against the window frame, lost in thought. "But before we drugged you. You had one right before that, didn't you? In the house." His eyes narrowed. "When Marco entered."

"And many others. You had an army with you, Cole."

"But-"

"It's not just Marco," I whispered, "it's never just been him."

He rubbed my leg in slow, steady strokes. "Maybe it's time to define what you call violent."

"And maybe it's not," I countered. "Cole, I know you are trying to help, and I appreciate that. I need that more than you know. But I did see my mother killed in my arms. She did bleed to death, gasping for breath, in my lap. I hear her last words echoing in my head at all times. All these flashbacks, whether they are real or imaginary, are merely competing in my scientific brain for some hierarchy of the awful events in my life. And thinking about them just makes them all come rushing back in a movie montage that is killing me. So, please-"

"Okay." His hands were on my face, wiping away the rush of frantic tears that were drenching me. "Ariana, I get it, and it's okay. Just breathe."

"God, I'm so fucking pathetic," I said through broken gasps. "Why can't I stop crying these days? Damn."

"You're not pathetic, Ariana. You're human. You've been thrown so much, so fast, I'd be worried if you weren't emotional. Add in some pretty damn brutal visions and I'm surprised you're still standing. No one, save a Valentine, could handle what you've been through."

"A lie, but a kind one," I murmured and gave him a half smile.

"It's hard for you, isn't it? To be here in the house?"

"Not the way you think. I have no memory of this place, so it's just another, house, another city like all the ones we've run to my whole life."

"Then what?"

"I don't know anyone here, Cole, and there's so much noise and chatter. My world before now was always calm. Just my mom and me, never getting close to hardly anyone else. We weren't quiet bookworms or nuns, obviously, but compared to this place; it was an oasis."

"And the memory flashes don't help that chaos, I'm sure. The sound of the ocean helps?"

"Not just the ocean but yes. It's a basic human response...repetitive sounds have a calming effect on the body's natural physical and chemical reactions."

"Fucking biochem. Priceless."

He'd lightened the mood in an instant, and I offered him a smile in thanks. "So, do you actually work or are you just a well-paid babysitter?"

"I earn my keep," he promised, "but I do have a commitment tonight actually."

"Other than me?"

"Yes, Ms. Valentine, other than you." He hesitated and tilted his head to the side. "But you can come if you like. Get you out of the house and into some repetitive rhythms anyway."

"Repetitive rhythms?" I laughed. "Did you just offer me repetitive rhythms, Cole?"

"Sounds. Repetitive sounds." He tapped my leg to get me to move. "Damn you have a filthy mind. Come on; you're gonna fit right in."

CHAPTER SIX

Finally. Something familiar. As soon as we stepped into the gun range, I felt at ease. There were a dozen or so Valentine men in their fancy suits but, knowing I'd have a gun in my hand soon; it didn't seem quite as threatening.

"Every few weeks we bring the guys out for some extra training. When it's slow, we do it more frequently just to keep them in practice."

"Wait...this is what you call slow?"

"It was slow until a random video got posted online and sent the entire family into crisis mode."

"So I'm a crisis," I frowned. "Good to know."

"Ariana-"

"Damn, Cole, don't be so sensitive. At least I'm a cute crisis, right?"

"Cute is not the word I would choose, no," one of the guys said, smiling as he took his gear off the desk.

"Cute is like for puppies or something," another interjected. "You're more like-"

Cole coughed. "The heir of the house of Valentine and therefore-"

"A beautiful, classy lady that we shall be honored to have with us this evening," another said, nodding. "Got it."

The group fell into laughter and Cole shook his head, turning back to me. "Have you ever shot before?"

I sent him a withering glance and waved him away from the desk. "Go be manly or whatever."

He chuckled and nodded to the attendant. "Give the lady something to start-"

"HK VP9, please."

"Alright, seems she's got this under control." Cole's brows furrowed together and he gave a mock bow. "Always a surprise, aren't you?"

I smiled. "I think I liked 'intoxicating' much better."

"Dangerous. Don't forget that part, Ariana," he chuckled.

"For such a fearless man, you can be incredibly cautious."

"Serrano, stop flirting and get over here!"

"Saved," I winked, "by the Valentine clan."

He moved into the shooting bays as I finished gathering up my things. Rather than jump right in, I hung in the periphery, watching the men take their turns. Cole seemed so animated - teaching, directing and ordering them but always in a manner that kept them relaxed and joking. They included me in their jokes whenever he was occupied with someone, and it made me feel like I actually belonged somewhere. I wondered if my mom had felt so comfortable with these men - or if their constant presence was what caused her to run.

Trying to shake off the melancholy I felt building; I took the next available bay. I'd been shooting for as long as I could remember and the gun felt weighty and familiar in my hand. Having something, anything really, familiar made my breaths calm and my head clear. I shot three of the four clips I'd been given before finally taking a break and motioning the range officer for a break. He retrieved my silhouette and placed it on the table with the others. I wasn't surprised when all the men crowded around to see how I did. They were complimentary - even though my groupings weren't nearly as tight as they should have been.

"Teresa taught you to shoot," Cole guessed.

I nodded. "It was a weekly ritual no matter where we lived."

He laid out one of his targets next to mine, a smile playing across his face. They were nearly identical - ten shots to the head, ten shots to the heart, ten shots to the abdomen...the pattern my mother had insisted upon. She'd obviously taught him the same benchmarks before we fled.

One of the men tapped our targets and then dropped a heavy arm around Cole's shoulders. "Like brother, like sister, right?"

An instant crimson blush heated my face, and I dropped my eyes away. Cole's throaty chuckle made it even worse as the men continued their ribbing. He took one long stride toward me, snaked a hand behind my head and pulled me into a fierce, unbreakable kiss. He stepped away and hit the man in the center of his chest with three sharp jabs. "Not *my* sister, brother."

The cat calls and whistles spread around the room and before I lost my nerve, I slinked up to Cole and grabbed the front of his jeans. I tugged his body into mine and, stretching on my toes, I put my lips close to his ear. "Ten for ten out of 100, big brother."

It was purposefully loud enough for everyone to hear and his head fell back in laughter. It was a challenge I knew he couldn't ignore with all of them watching.

"Load and reset us, boys."

"A Valentine challenge? Who'll give me a $100 on Cole?"

"Nah, he'll throw it for her-"

The bets were flying, the testosterone building, and I couldn't help but feel alive again. Their camaraderie was infectious.

"You good?"

"I'm fine, Cole."

"They haven't been like this in ages. So thank you for that."

"Let's see how much you thank me when I kick your ass."

"We're set." The range officer extended his hand toward the bay. "Ladies first."

"Hell, no." I shook my head. "He doesn't get the chance to miss on purpose just to let me win."

"Cole never misses on purpose," one called.

A snort from somewhere in the group. "Have you seen her legs?"

He gave me a quick wink before tugging his earmuffs back on. He stepped to the line and fired his ten shots in rapid succession without a single hesitation.

"99."

"Damn, Cole. Not gonna leave her any wiggle room?"

To his credit, he did offer me an apologetic grin as he moved aside so I could take my turn. I took a deep breath and had cycled through nine slow shots before having to stop and readjust.

"Tied at 90 with one shot remaining for Ms. Valentine."

I glared at the range officer. "But no pressure, right?"

I felt Cole warm behind me, his lips tracing down my neck, his fingers following a sexy trail down my spine. He gave a low chuckle that sent shivers down to my toes.

"Sorry, gotta preserve my reputation here."

I tilted my head over my shoulder and wiggled my eyebrows. "Desperate much?"

He smiled, his lips returning to my throat, as the men started barking to distract me. I glanced up, locking my gaze with his...and then fired.

Cole's eyes jerked to the target, but I turned in his arms and gave him a quick kiss on the jaw.

"100," I whispered, just as the range officer confirmed my hit.

Cole was rushed by the men, a rash of good-natured insults assaulting him.

"All right, all right!" He finally held up his hands. "Get your gear and get over to the bar. Drinks are on Ms. Valentine tonight."

I nodded at their appreciation as they gathered gear and headed out. The range officer handed me my target, already rolled into a tight cylinder.

Cole and his two shadows remained, straightening up the mess that had been left behind.

"Despite the shit, I'm getting from the guys, I've gotta give it to you. That was pretty fucking impressive."

"Guess that Serrano charm can't match her Valentine skills tonight, Cole."

"Fuck you, Tony," he laughed. "But yes. It seems she is immune to my touch, doesn't it?"

I tapped the target on Cole's chest, offering him a tiny wink. "Memento?"

He paused, confused, and then unrolled the paper and spread it on the table. My first nine were dead on but the last, the one where he'd distracted me, was so far off center it didn't even hit the silhouette.

He frowned and sent me a quizzical glance. "90?"

"I bribed the range officer."

It took a minute for them to understand and then they all began shaking with laughter.

"Now that," he grinned, draping his arm over my shoulders, "was the move of a true fucking Valentine."

CHAPTER SEVEN

While my jeans and tank top fit in at the gun range; I was totally out of place at the "bar." To me, a bar was a tiki hut with a sand floor where tourists gathered in front for fluorescent drinks while the rest of us bought whiskey out of a side window. For the Valentine men, bar apparently meant the high rollers VIP lounge at the nearby casino. No one seemed to care about my attire except me and, after making friends with the bartender, I took several drinks in quick succession to stop caring myself.

Cole and his musketeers had watched me on the dance floor for over an hour before either deciding I was safe enough, or getting bored of my twirling. They retreated to a quiet table in the corner and started holding court as snappy looking men and scantily clad women paraded to them. For some reason, it absolutely infuriated me, and I moved beyond the safety of the VIP Lounge to the throbbing main club. Here, everything was wilder, faster, and much more risqué. Trying to forget everything, I pretended to be someone else and flung myself in the hardest, darkest center of it.

A half hour later, as I was fighting a really cocky but well-dressed man in the middle of the floor, a soft tug at my elbow broke us apart and began leading me back to the VIP Lounge. Apparently, my escape was acceptable but fighting the clientele was forbidden. I didn't know the man leading me which was terrifying, but at least I knew he was leading me to safety which was what I needed more than anything. My emotions began to skitter out of control, and I tried to pull myself together.

"Did you get lost, Ariana?" Cole asked, without looking my direction.

"Don't send a stranger to get me ever again."

Something in my voice made all the men turn my direction. Cole motioned for space, and the table cleared instantly, leaving nothing but his shadows.

"My apologies."

"Can I ask you something? All of you?" I dropped heavily into the cushions.

"Can you?" Al asked, pushing a glass of water my direction.

I nodded my thanks and swallowed several gulps while balancing my other glass in my hand. "You are a bunch of good looking guys, right? I mean, all of you are damn cocky about it, so it's not as if I'm telling you anything new."

Tony leaned forward, eying me closely. "Just how much have you had to drink?"

"She'd say that sober; I assure you."

"I'm kinda starting to love her, Cole."

"You all have that sexy, danger thing going on. You all carry guns, you all dress impeccably well…"

"Ariana."

"Stop staring at me, Cole. I'm not trying to be a smartass. I'm asking with complete candidness."

"Candidness?" Al asked, raising an eyebrow. "Is that even a word?"

"Yes. My point is, you can pretty much get a girl at any time, right? If you go home alone, it's by choice, right?"

"How much *have* you had to drink?"

"Just two. It's probably the GHB which is..."

"What?"

"Wait, what-"

My eyes darted to each of them who were now sitting up and staring at me. "Which is my question. With everything you guys have going for you, why is it necessary to spike a girl's drink in hopes of getting laid?"

Cole and Tony were beside me instantly, caging me into the cushions. Cole was checking my wrist and Tony was trying to take my drink out of my other hand.

"Give me the glass, kid."

"I'm not done."

"Ariana, give him the fucking glass."

I took a long gulp and then handed it off. "So... why is it necessary?"

"I fully intend to get laid tonight. Do you see me spiking any drinks here?" Tony asked as he sniffed the glass. "How do you know it's GHB?"

I shrugged. "It just is."

"We keep a test kit behind the bar," Al provided. "I'll go grab it."

"Cole, my heart rate is a million times better than yours right now so will you just stop?" I jerked my arm away from his grasp. I closed my eyes trying to stave off the memories that were starting to leak back into my psyche.

"Ariana, look at me."

Al tossed the test kit at Tony. I could hear them moving about, but I just couldn't bring myself to care.

"She's right. It's positive. How the hell could she know that?"

"It's salty," I murmured. "Unless you add lemon juice or something else acidic, it's salty."

"Again, how the fuck does she know that?"

"Ariana-" Cole demanded.

"Just talk to me, okay? It's hard to focus, and I need to focus on something." I took his hand and pulled it to rest on top of my thigh, rubbing it back and forth. "I'll burn it off in fifteen minutes but, please, just distract me until then."

"How about I distract you by kicking his fucking ass?"

"Cole, take a look at her, brother."

"Ariana, do you know who did it?"

"Of course. The big guy with the sapphire tie...the one with tiny fleur-de-lis."

"Get him."

"Cole-"

"I know, Tony, I know! Just find him. As soon as he learns her name, he'll be running. Get to him first."

"I miss her so much."

Cole's hands were soft on me, shuffling me to stretch out and lay my head in his lap. His hand drifted to my stomach, his thumb making tight circles on my ribs.

"Your touch makes it better," I murmured.

"I think that's the liquid X talking, baby girl."

"It's not fair you keep telling me no because I'm a stupid Valentine. I didn't even know I was a Valentine, and I have extremely happy memories of your hands but nothing else in my whole life is happy and-"

"I know you don't mean to say that out loud in a public place."

"No, sorry, I'm not." I shook my head trying to get my thoughts in some sort of order. "It's a power thing, isn't it? Slipping the drug to women? It's not as if they are hard up."

"Yes, it is. How bad are your memories swirling right now?"

"They aren't. I'm fine."

"Ariana," he murmured, "you haven't stopped crying since you first sat down at the table."

My hands flashed to my face and, sure enough, I was drenched with tears. I frowned. I'd really thought I'd been holding it together. "Do all of you pharmaceutical drug dealer type people just carry random drugs around in your pocket? Is this something I have to look forward to every fucking day?"

"No, we don't. At least not in the Valentine family. It's something we'll have to watch for, though. Your system reacts differently."

"My system reacts just as it should. It's the suppression of brain function," I argued. "For everyone else, it makes things happy and euphoric. For me, it means I can't consciously block out all the things I need to block out."

I could hear someone join us and knew it had to be the bigger guy, the fun one... Tony, I reminded myself. "Did the girl high on X just break down the human physiological effects of a drug?"

"Biochem major," Cole chuckled.

"Seriously? That's priceless."

"Fuck you," I grumbled.

"Did you find him?"

"Yeah. We've got him in a back room. Cole, he's a Valentine."

I could feel Cole's entire body tense beneath me. "Not any-more," he hissed. "Remove his brand and get him the hell out of here."

"I'll have it taken care of."

"How much longer?" I whimpered.

"Too long," Cole said, shuffling me in his lap. "Repetitive sounds, did you say? Or something to focus on?"

I nodded.

"Tony, gather up some glasses for me, would you? Spike some of them with whatever you can buy off the assholes here, and then you and Al come back, all right?"

"Cole, are they gone?"

"Temporarily."

"How could you...I mean, men have come for me my whole entire life...how could you...why would you ever send a stranger to get me?"

"Ariana, I'm so sorry. I didn't even think-"

"Why haven't you asked about the memories this time?"

"Because I know you'd tell me, baby girl. The drug doesn't give a damn what you want to keep private, but I do. Come on, sit up. We're going to play a game."

"Childish."

"Okay, a test. Is that better?"

Tony and the other shadow were back, lining up a set of glasses along the drink table. They ranged from icy blue to glowing green with a few coffee colored ones thrown in. Once they were laid out, the men dropped to sit across from us.

"Is my test not to pass out after drinking all this shit?"

"If you can do that, I'm stealing you away from him," Tony laughed. "What are we doing here, Cole?"

"Ariana, tell me if any of these are spiked and, if you can, what's in them."

"Cole that is-" the quiet one was protesting.

I found his soft indignation hysterical and began laughing. "No, no. It's okay. Great actually. I can do this. Focus," I smiled and squeezed Cole's hand before picking up the first glass.

I swirled it, smelled it and then pushed it back. "Ketamine."

"Correct."

I picked up the second glass and only had to smell it before passing it back. "LSD."

"Correct."

The third was dark, almost syrupy and I frowned at the smell of it. I stuck my pinky in it, tasted it, and then my eyes narrowed. "You know this kind of soda isn't actually made of cocaine, right? Not spiked."

Tony laughed so hard it made his body shake, and I knew I was going to love him.

"Correct."

"Xanax, really?" I grumbled on the next. "Who carries Xanax to a club?"

"Tourists."

"Fucking tourists," I whispered but my entire body spasmed and Cole's hand was fast on my waist. The other men were laughing, they hadn't noticed my reaction, and I fought to control the memories from the night of the bonfire.

"Ariana-"

I offered him a halfhearted smile. "Last one, right?" I picked up the glass and swirled it, smelled it, tasted a pinky full and still couldn't find anything. "Not spiked." Confident, I took the shot down in one swallow just as Tony and Al both lunged for me.

I was wrong. I was so fucking wrong.

My brain launched into a full mental seizure, flashes of memories, lights, places and people colliding in rapid fire succession.

"What the hell is that?" Cole's arms were around me, gripping me tight to his chest, but I was struggling...and winning.

"Modafinil, isolated for Valentine." Same calm, reasonable voice as always.

"Of all the choices..."

I could hear Cole's voice but didn't care. I broke free of his grasp, grabbing my head and rushing toward the exit. They were on my heels fast, wrenching me back, but the music and noise made everything a technicolor swirl, and I dropped to my knees.

"Beach, please," I begged.

I was over Tony's shoulder in seconds, closing my eyes as the world began to spin with all the movement. I felt his steps stumble as we hit the sand across the Boardwalk and then he sat me down. Cole knelt in front of me, cupping my face in his hands.

"Ariana, look at me. Look at me!"

"Cole, what the hell-"

"Coffee," he ordered, "find her coffee."

"The last thing a Modafinil overdose needs is caffeine," Al offered.

"She's not like others. Get the damn coffee."

"Cole," I whimpered. I dropped my head between my knees, clenching my skull as the visions kept coming. "I can't make them stop."

"Tony, how long?"

"She burned the liquid X off in half the time so, three hours maybe?"

"She'll be suicidal in five minutes," Cole spat, rubbing my arms up and down as if trying to keep me warm. "Ariana, baby girl…"

His pleading tone caused my eyes to open. He looked so broken and helpless…and angry. He was so very angry. I touched my hand to his face, stroking his cheek. "Don't be mad. Please don't be mad."

"I'm not mad," he promised, but I didn't believe a word of it.

I turned in the sand, grabbing Tony's pants legs. "Tony."

He dropped down to my level, and I smiled. "He's wrong, isn't he? You do carry drugs with you. You have to. Just in case."

"I don't-"

I tugged on him again, my tears now desperate. "Tony, please-"

"Yes."

"Lorazepam?"

"What's she talking about?"

"It's in clinical trials as an overdose treatment. No fucking clue how she knows that, though."

"Half lora, half diphenhydramine."

"Do you have it?"

"It's in trials, Cole. It might work, or it might just drop her into a fucking coma."

"Tony, do you have it or not?"

"Yes. The shop right there should have generic diphen."

"I'll get it. Dose her the lora."

"Cole-" Tony tried, but he was already gone. He turned dark eyes my direction. "Is whatever flooding your head really bad enough to chance killing yourself?"

I took his hand, squeezing it as hard as I could. "Yes."

He tipped my chin up, letting a finger drift down my hair as he stared at me with an intensity that left me feeling like my entire soul was completely exposed. He nodded as he reached some decision that was, thankfully, in my favor. "You're going to-"

"Pass out, I know," I murmured, dropping my head back down against my legs and starting to rock myself. "I promise, I'm am 500% okay with that, Tony."

"How the hell do you know all this, kid? It's not in a textbook and you damn sure aren't an addict."

I shook my head, willing Cole to move faster before I started saying the things teeming through my head.

"Here," Tony tucked a pill into my hand. "Al here has the coffee or Cole will bring water-"

I downed it dry and went back to rocking. It seemed like hours but Cole was back minutes later, ripping open the medicine and handing me two pills. I swallowed them with the water this time and then looked at all of them. "He killed them did you know? Did all of you know and just not want to say anything?"

"What?"

"Franco, my father. He strangled them both while I was-"

Cole's lips were soft on mine, cutting off my words. "Quiet, Ariana. You need to be silent now."

It was an order, and I nodded in obedience.

"Let's get her to the house."

"Cole?" I asked, quiet as a mouse as someone lifted me off the ground. "How do you remove a brand?"

"We burn it out of his fucking flesh, kid."

CHAPTER EIGHT

I awoke to soft caresses stroking the length of my body, the smell of seawater enrobing me like a comforting blanket. Considering the night I'd had, it was already starting off to be a much better day. I was stretched on top of Cole, but we weren't on the bed. My eyes drifted around, trying to place our location, and then realized we were on the sofa in the room they claimed was mine. I turned my head, ever so slightly against his chest, and met his intense gaze.

"Good morning again."

His warm, husky voice sent shivers down my body, and he gave a low chuckle.

"Again?"

"You woke up about ten minutes ago and climbed on me before falling back asleep. I must admit, it was a delightful way to be awoken."

I nodded but made no move to leave. My body was chilled, my camisole and underwear offering little protection, but each of his long strokes against my skin was leaving a soothing warmth behind.

"Are you feeling alright? No after effects or anything? Hangover?"

"A little sore, bruised maybe, but otherwise good."

"We had to get a little rough with you in the club, do you remember? It was like fighting a fucking tiger."

"They don't call it the super soldier drug for no reason."

"Do you remember?" he repeated.

"Which answer do you want?"

"The truthful one."

"Yes, Cole. I remember." I shuffled my hands loose, reaching to trace his jawline. His hands stopped moving, and I gave him a challenging smile. "If you can explore, so can I."

"Fair enough," he murmured, his hands once again traveling my curves. "How much?"

"Everything until the lora."

"Did you know he had spiked the drink before you drank it?"

"No. I asked for water because it was so hot on the dance floor. I guzzled it and realized about halfway through."

"Don't ever do that again. If you'd taken two seconds to check it, you would've known it was spiked. Did you call him on it? Is that why you were fighting on the dance floor?"

"Yes and he admitted it. Gloated about it actually."

I shuffled up a tiny fraction on his chest and began running my lips along his neck. Rather than stop me, as I expected, Cole's hands locked on my hips, and he murmured "lift up a sec." I did as told, and he scooted himself lower on the sofa, allowing me to feel the entire length of him against my body: my breasts heavy against his chest; my nipples growing hard from the weight of our bodies together; how his breaths were becoming more shallow; his cock twitching hard between my thighs even with jeans keeping it contained.

"You have a lot of assholes working for you."

"Usually they're pretty above board. I'm sorry that you seem to be finding the less than stellar ones. I wouldn't advise you to keep trying to fight them, though. They are extraordinarily well trained." His palms slipped to my ass, cupping it, tightening and releasing it a sliding rhythm that made my insides twitch in a way I'd never felt before. "Anything else?"

"That I remember?" I asked, struggling to keep my mind on the conversation. "I told you. I remember the test, the beach until I passed out."

"The memories, Ariana."

"Oh." I let out a little shiver.

"That's a yes," he murmured, his lips pressing into my neck and causing my body to arch against him. My movement was so quick, so harsh, that he reacted instinctively. His hips followed mine, thrusting toward me as his hand tangled in my hair and pulled me into a fierce kiss. His lips were everywhere all at once, and his ragged breath was fast turning into a low moan. His fingers moved back around my ass, sliding between my thighs and I knew he could feel the slickness already seeping down. "Christ," he groaned and rocked himself hard against me. "Ariana," he called, his words a near beg at my throat, "baby girl, I need you to stop us because I can't."

Need. Somehow that word registered hard in my brain...he needed us to stop not *wanted* us to stop. I nodded, still breathless but I shuffled off him to sit at the edge of the sofa. We sat still for several minutes, neither of us moving, as we tried to get ourselves back in control. He was first to recover and moved to sit on the table across from me. His fingers drifted to my cheek, feather light, and then pulled me into a gentle, tame kiss. His lips were soft against mine, his words full of gratitude. "Thank you," he whispered.

He stood up and went to the dresser, retrieving me a bottle of water. After I'd drank down half, he smiled. "Better?"

I nodded and returned the smile, but I wasn't okay. I'd never felt anything like him before; my body had never wanted anything like it wanted him...and yet he kept turning me away. It was devastating..and totally embarrassing.

"Ariana?" he asked, worried.

I nodded again. "You were asking about the memories."

"Well, yes and no. I admit I'm damn curious who Franco was strangling in front of you."

I shifted, trying to curl in on myself but his hand on my leg stopped me.

"Please stop trying to hide from me."

"I said that?"

"Yes, but I'm not asking about what they are since I told you I wouldn't. Instead, I want to know about the drugs. How did you know all of that information? Tony's right. Your knowledge is way beyond something a school would ever teach you."

"I wish I could tell you, Cole, but I really don't know. I just knew them like a person knows how to breathe."

He hesitated for the briefest moment and then leaned forward to kiss my forehead. "Okay then. I'd like your help with something this morning if you don't mind."

"A project? Awesome." I side-stepped him, grabbed my jeans and tugged them over my legs. I continued to rush around the room, gathering my things.

"I sense a bit of pent-up energy," he chuckled.

"Fuck you, Cole," I grumbled. "Blame the drug cocktail from last night. I'd probably be sulking otherwise."

"Sulking?" he reached from behind me, buttoning my jeans for me. "I don't believe that's the emotion I've been seeing."

I batted his hands away. "You know what I mean."

"I do," he chuckled, "but you may not be so excited when you see the project. Meet me in the kitchen and I'll pay you in coffee."

"Deal."

"And remind me to have Bridgett get you some more clothes. You've been wearing the same thing for days now."

I turned in his arms, my fingers tracing his chest as seductively as I could manage without laughing. "I could always just go naked."

"Yeah, the boys would love that. And then I'd have to kill them."

"Go on," I pushed him away, "make me coffee."

"So bossy," he said, winking as he left the room.

I looked around and realized he was right about the clothes. I only had what my mother and I had managed to stuff in the duffel before we left. Seeing a notepad on the table, I jotted down a few things along with my sizes. Bridgett had an uncanny knack for choosing well, but I really wanted comfort clothes: sweats and a giant oversized tee-shirt. I brushed my teeth and then went to join Cole in the kitchen.

"Why does it smell like a florist shop in here?" I asked, screwing up my nose.

He nodded toward the hallway beyond. "We'd asked the shop to hold off on delivering the memorial flowers but, after last night, they ran out of space."

I stuck my head into the hallway. There were hundreds of arrangements in different sizes and colors, tucked in every corner of the space. I took a step back, covering my nose. "That is nauseating."

"You have a very acute sense of smell," he observed, watching me. "Like a sommelier or a perfumer."

"Stop analyzing me. Can we open windows or something? Doors?"

"I've got men coming to move them over to the church. They'll be gone soon."

"What did you mean, until last night?"

"Hm?" He put the coffee tin back and pulled mugs out. "Oh, last night. The guys inundated the florist with orders."

I had no idea what the hell he was talking about, and my patience was wearing thin as the flower smells burned into my nose. "Cole."

He glanced up from his doings and, seeing my annoyance flaring, he frowned. Reaching over the sink, he flung open the windows to get more air circulating. "The Valentine men were distraught about what happened to you at the club last night. They sent flowers in apology."

"Apologize for what? Because some asshole put something in my drink?"

"Because another Valentine had the audacity to do such a thing because they didn't learn about it in time to prevent it because they failed to protect you because they didn't get to exact their own justice because you are you."

"That is too much guilt for one person's brain," I grumbled. "I fucking hate flowers."

"I'll make sure to let them know. Now," his hand reached to my jeans, tugging me closer. "I may not be as observant as you, but I know that somewhere we stepped over the sexually frustrated emotion into something else. So, will you please tell me what's really the matter?"

"It's just the flowers," I assured him. "It's the oldest memory I have. I woke up, covered in a pink daisy blanket, in a flower stall at the French Market in New Orleans."

"Where was Teresa?"

"She was there, talking to some men but I didn't know that for a few minutes. I thought I was all alone in this strange place with so many smells and colors. She scooped me in her arms but only after I started screaming." I smiled to reassure him. "It just sets my nerves on edge. I'll be fine once it airs out."

"And if you just tell me," he grumbled, "I can fix it for you." He kissed the top of my head and stepped toward the hallway, calling out one of the men I hadn't even noticed. "Get the flowers out on the street. They can load them from there. Refuse any future deliveries and send them straight to the church."

"Yes, sir."

He stepped back toward me, touching my hand just to get me to look at him. "Ariana, I *am* sorry about sending him to get you. I had no idea...no, that's not true. If I'd taken the time to think, I would've realized how idiotic sending some muscled up guy in a dark suit with a gun was, but I didn't think. I just wanted you off that floor, safe and back with us. I am truly sorry. As it turned out, I probably should have made that call a lot earlier, but I wanted you to have some semblance of freedom."

"You didn't take away my freedom, Cole. I've never really had any." I pushed a slip of paper his direction. "Things I could use. I made a list. If it's too much-"

He gave me a withering look and sat it on the counter without bothering to read it. "She'll have it here within the hour."

I nodded, watching as coffee began to gurgle through a pipe of the tiny Bialetti. It was battered and tarnished, the little man icon barely visible...just like the one my mother had been using all my life. "By the way, has there been any news about my father?"

He handed me a steaming mug then leaned back against the counter. "That's the first time you've asked."

"I hear enough, Cole. He learned about my mother, had a very public meltdown, and now while you men plan her memorial with Father Michael, was it? He's avoiding the world. Including me."

"You are way too observant for this household," he grumbled. "He's fine. Well, not fine, but safe. He won't return until he can face everyone with no weakness. Especially you. Being strong for us, for you...that's who he is."

I nodded, not exactly believing, but knew I wasn't going to get any further explanation. I took a long draft of the coffee. "Your coffee is divine."

"And you are instantly a much happier person," he observed.

"It covers the smell of the flowers," I grinned, smiling over my cup. "My mom's was always sweet."

"Sweet espresso?" he grimaced. "Can't imagine how you ever got addicted to that."

"The one addiction to which I succumbed. Not bad considering the other choices out there."

"Oh, I think you've found yet another," he murmured, giving me a quick kiss on my throat. "Come on, time to earn our paychecks."

CHAPTER NINE

He pointed to the dining room, grabbing his coffee and following behind. His two shadows were already there, sitting in chairs, drinking their own coffee and I gave them a little wave. Both smiled with a polite "Morning, Ms. Valentine," which made me giggle. Moving past them, I circled the table and gave a low whistle. Lined up on the polished mahogany were hundreds of vials. Some were liquid, others solid, all ranging from clear to pristine white.

"It looks like my old high school chemistry lab."

"Then your school must've been a hell of a lot more fun than mine was."

I frowned at them but then understanding washed over me. I shook my head at my own idiocy. "They're all illegal."

"No. Some are legal, even if just barely," Cole explained. "But, yes, they are controlled substances."

"So, are you guys throwing a party or what?"

They were laughing again, and warmth swelled inside me. They were so easy, so relaxed and fun. How had I missed this side of all of them? Is that what having a family was really like?

"Like I said, we need your help." He motioned to the men. "Your tolerance or immunity or whatever the hell it is has everyone confused, and your ability to discern recipes has put us all on edge. I'm not really going to explain why it's so important, so I need you just to accept that it is."

I shrugged. I didn't care at all why they were worried about it. I was holding firm to the idea that the less I knew about the Valentine family, the less I had to admit what type of bad things they were involved in. "Okay, so what do you need from me?"

"There are 216 different substances here. I want you to tell us what they are."

"I am not stupid enough to ingest random drugs on your whim. We went there already...it didn't end well if you remember."

"She's got you there, Cole."

He sent a strangling look that stopped the man cold. "Tell me what you can *without* ingesting them and then we'll see what's left."

"Just so you know, I excel at tests." I dropped into the first chair and sat my coffee down. "Are there any I can't taste?"

Cole opened his mouth, but one of the men stopped him. Grinning, he handed me a vial. "You tell us."

"You, Tony, are having way too much fun with this."

"Guilty as charged," he laughed. "We have few diversions these days."

I examined the vial...shaking it, pouring a tiny amount into my hand and pushing it around. I sniffed it and immediately recoiled. "I will not be tasting that," I grumbled. "White gunpowder."

"No, it's-"

"Potassium nitrate and powdered sugar also known as white gunpowder. It was used in the Civil War when supplies of regular gunpowder ran low."

"Well, shit," Tony grumbled but gave me a wink. "I'll refill that coffee for you."

Cole's eyes lifted to the other man, the quieter one. "Al, is she right?"

"Yeah, she's right."

I was ten for ten before one finally stumped me. No matter what I tried, nothing about the substance stood out to me. I put it aside, frustrated, but determined to come back to it later. Every answer I got right earned praise from Al and Tony while Cole's mood grew darker and darker. As we hit seventy-five and another drug I couldn't identify, Cole shot out of his seat, startling us all. The other men took a step back, recognizing his emotions instantly, but it took me a moment to place it: fury. He was fucking livid.

"Lunch. DeSalvo's." Clipped orders that the men followed without question. Al and Tony each took one of my arms, a light touch to direct me. They led me in silence, out of the house and two blocks down the road. Cole was there, paces behind, never saying a word. We entered the tiny restaurant and were greeted with an onslaught of hugs and kisses on the cheek. It was obviously their regular hangout, and they'd been missed while they were babysitting me.

Al and Tony lightened the mood, flirting with the waitresses and sharing stories of misadventures they had at the place. I couldn't remember the last time I'd eaten, and I devoured everything, earning a friendly ribbing from them. Through it all, Cole's silence bore down on me, a weight that wouldn't lift no matter how they made me laugh.

When we returned to the house, I headed back to the dining room, taking my seat. I was determined not to let Cole's mood infect the rest of us, and I clapped my hand on the table. "Bartender, another round!"

Al and Tony laughed but, as one handed me a vial, Cole's hand blocked them. "Stop. There's no point. She'll know them all."

"But-"

Cole checked the list and searched the table before pulling out a single vial and handing it to me. I took it, felt a confusing sense of pressure to identify this one but somehow knowing I wouldn't be able to. I tried, longer than I'd given any of the other vials, and he finally took it out of my hands.

"Except these." He laid it out perfect in front of me, taking the time to straighten it and align it with the edge of the table. "Rohypnol." He picked up the first vial I'd saved for later inspection and laid it next to the other. "Ecstasy." He reached for the third, lining it up, but I felt the knot well in my stomach.

"Modafinil," I whispered.

"Modafinil," he hissed. His arms swung wide, sending vials flying across the room and shattering against the wall. When he realized he'd missed a few, he did it again. When the table was clear except for a sprinkling of powders, he gripped the edge, his muscles twitching as his temper raged out of control. Al and Tony had taken up protective stances on either side of me, but it was unnecessary - Cole was calming himself with every breath. When he had settled enough to drop into a chair, Al and Tony did the same.

"You are certain that all this time, all these years, it's been just you and your mother?"

"I'm certain."

"Do not lie to me. Not now."

I fought down the indignation of his question. "I'm not."

"Ariana," his voice was a low gravel, the one he used when we were alone, "look at me."

I obeyed just as he knew I would.

"There's been no one else? A friend, a regular visitor, a lover?"

"No, Cole. No one."

His hands went to his hair, raking through it twice. They moved to his face, rubbing his jaw - a personal tic of his I'd already memorized. It meant nothing good was about to happen, and I curled my legs up into the chair, waiting.

He exhaled in a last effort to calm his voice. "No human is born to know these things, Ariana. We have hundreds of highly educated pharmacists in our employ, and none could do what you just did."

"Like the Valentine drug, I'm a freak. Thanks."

"No," Tony offered me a half smile. "A heroin addict will know heroin but not meth. A cocaine addict will recognize his drug but have no clue about another you set in front of him. He'll know it's not his, but that's it."

"I can assure you; I'm not addicted to any of this shit."

"No one is saying you are," Al interjected. "But you have been trained, conditioned, whatever word you want to use, to recognize hundreds of mind-altering substances."

"No, I-"

"If you walked into a bar and some guy tried to drop something in your drink, you'd know. No one would have a chance to get one over on you."

Tony snorted. "If she bothered to check anyway."

"Say that again," Cole commanded, leaning forward.

"If she walked into a bar-"

"No, the last part. What did you say?"

"No one will have a chance to get one over on her."

He laughed, a deep throaty laugh that caused us all to face him. "I'll say it a thousand times. Teresa was fucking brilliant." He smiled at me, still chuckling. "It wasn't someone else."

"I told you that."

He gave me an apologetic grin. "It was her all along. She conditioned you to know them. She was protecting you, Ariana."

"From what?"

"The families," Tony answered. "When everyone moved into pharmaceuticals as the main business, each took their spin on the drug trade. All of these we had in front of you are components used by different families, including ours. Since you can recognize them, they'd never have a chance to slipping something to you that would allow you to be kidnapped."

"Or killed," Al added.

"Well, unless they decide to give me the ever popular and readily available date-rape drug, as we've already established. Then, I'm just shit out of luck."

Cole nodded. "She has a point. She can recognize the Valentine drug components when they are mixed but not separately."

"She," I grumbled, "is right here."

But Cole was in his thinking mode and ignored me. "Why would she do that?" he asked himself. "What did she hope to accomplish?"

"Maybe she thought I didn't need to be protected from my own fucking family?"

The men exchanged glances, but it was Al's quiet voice that finally responded. "Teresa, of anyone, knew better than that."

Irritation and frustration washed over me at the cryptic discussion. I hopped out of the chair, treading to the other room and then coming back with a bottle of whiskey and a stack of glasses. I spread them out, pouring some for each, and then circled the table to deliver them before settling in the chair next to Cole.

Al gave me an apologetic smile. "On duty, but thank you."

"Valentine, right?" I growled, pointing at myself. "Put someone else on duty and have a damn drink."

"God, I love her, Cole," Tony laughed and downed his drink in a swallow before pouring himself another.

"Stupid name has to be good for something."

Cole nodded to Al. "You heard the lady. Make it happen."

Al nodded and swallowed his drink before slipping out the door to order more troops. Or whatever he intended to do. I didn't even care anymore.

"What's the street value?"

"You mean before Cole busted it all to shit? $2.3 million."

Millions? I lived in a world of fast food burgers, city bus transport, and store brand Keds. They had just destroyed something worth more than everything I'd owned in my life. I shook my head. "Valentine. What's it's street value?"

"It's not sold in market," Cole answered.

*In market....*as if we were talking about the grocery store. "But if you knew the recipe. How much would the components be?"

I could see Tony squint as he tried to do the math in his head. "Two hundred, maybe? For, a half dose not including the labor to make it."

"That's one hell of an expensive habit."

Tony nodded. "A hundred grand a year, easy, considering the fluctuations in supply and demand of the component drugs."

Cole's eyes were on me, evaluating. "Why?"

"Just curious."

"Your curiosity is a frightening thing to ponder," Cole mumbled. "Tony, you want to get someone in here to clean this up before you drink us all under the table?"

"Yes, sir. Be right back."

"Sorry for being bossy," I mumbled as Cole and I were left alone.

"It *is* your birthright. Sexy little girl bossing around grown men. They loved it." His hand moved to the back of my chair, his fingers drifting across the back of my neck. "Just don't think about trying that on me."

His touch was feather light against my skin, dipping along the curves of my shoulders and trailing up each side of my throat.

"Are you doing that on purpose?" I purred.

His eyes darted to me at the sound, and his movements stopped. "No, I hadn't realized. My apologies."

He drew his hand away, wrapping it safely around his glass. "Like a fucking magnet," he grumbled, low under his breath.

I decided it was best to let that comment pass. "You seem to trust them."

"I do," he nodded, sipping his drink. "They loved your mother."

As if that answered everything. I shook my head and decided drinking was a much better avenue than conversation.

"So it's not just tequila you love," he said. "Any alcohol will suffice?"

"These days? Yes."

"You can't drown away the truth, Ariana."

"A drug dealer is not allowed to give me advice on substance abuse. Do *not* lecture me."

He nodded. "We develop and traffic not deal, but fair enough."

"You were so angry."

"I'd apologize, but I did warn you about my temper."

"It's not that," I said, shaking my head. "I still don't understand why."

"It never occurred to me that your mother had been drugging you. I assumed someone else, someone not a Valentine, had been in your life."

"My mother did not-"

"Ariana."

"She wouldn't have," I protested.

"You can't have it both ways. Either there was someone in your lives, with regular access to you for over a decade and you are lying about it, or it was Teresa."

"You think I'm lying to you?"

"No, Ariana, I don't," he said, his voice patient and soothing. "I think you've lost your mother, and you desperately want to believe that she had no dark side."

"My mom was a good person."

"Yes, she was, but everyone has a dark side. That she used that to protect you? It's nothing to get defensive about."

Tony and Al were back, moving to clean up the mess Cole had made. I watched them for a moment, mixed emotions raging through me. "But how could she without me knowing? I mean, the history, scientific stuff we talked about at dinner. I loved science, and it was just conversation… something we had in common but to recognize them? It's not as if I sat down at a table and she fed me drugs."

He gave my shoulder a reassuring squeeze. "That is something we'll try and figure out."

"And the money. My mom was working as a pharmacy tech with a GED. The money you guys are talking about was way, way out of her league."

Cole hesitated, long enough for me to turn to look at him. But when he opened his mouth to reply, Tony was quick to cut him off. "How do you two feel about dinner? Wine, music, my homemade red sauce?"

Al smiled. "Kristina would love to meet you."

"His wife," Cole provided. "She seven months pregnant and loves anything that gets her out of the house. Al has her going stir crazy."

"Yeah," he grinned, "locking her away like someone else I know."

"Point taken," Cole grumbled and glanced at me. "You up for company?"

I nodded, aggravated by the whole veiled attempt to steer me onto another subject. "One last night of freedom before my father arrives, hm? Can't wait for that."

Cole shot a quizzical glance at the men.

Tony nodded. "We just got word. He'll touchdown around eight tomorrow morning."

"How did you know that?"

I shrugged.

"Ariana."

I huffed and pointed through the doorway where the access panel was in full view. "I saw them changing the alarm codes. You didn't tell them to; I didn't tell them to, so…"

"That only leaves your father." Cole's voice held an emotion I didn't recognize, and I glanced his way. The men had some non-verbal sparring match, and I sighed, taking a drink to try and ignore them.

"There is something else," Al mumbled. His arm waved to the pile of shattered vials. "Her ability-"

But Cole was already nodding. "Is invaluable. I know. Get another six men on the perimeter and one on each door."

"I'm going to the beach," I announced to no one in particular.

"No-" Al started to protest.

"I'm going to the beach," I repeated, pushing away from the table. "You do whatever you have to do."

"Such a spitfire," Tony chuckled.

I was already heading upstairs when the response finally came. It was cold, furious, and not the least bit amused. "Call in another twelve."

CHAPTER TEN

How long have you been out here?"

"I'm sure you already know the answer to that."

"Yes, I do," he admitted. "You've sat out here through the rain storm, while the temperature dropped, and now you're half frozen. Come inside."

"I'm fine."

"If you won't worry about yourself then think about Charlie."

"Who the hell is Charlie?"

"He's the sniper sitting guard on the roof. Through the same rain and the same temperature drop because you are being too fucking childish to go inside."

I stood up with as much grace I could manage and stalked past him. "Don't you ever call me childish."

He was at my heels, quiet steps that barely registered in my head. "Ariana-"

"No, there's nothing I want to hear right now."

"Your family-"

I whirled on him, nearly colliding with his chest. I looked up at him, my voice quiet. "Family? You mean my mother. The only person in my life. The woman I trusted so completely that I've followed her blindly from one town to the other. For what? Just so she could continue to use me as a fucking lab rat. My father. Who doesn't even bother to talk to me on the phone after fifteen years, knowing that my mother, his wife, bled to death in my arms? And then there's your precious house of Valentine. Who learns of my drug knowledge and then decides I'm some fucking commodity to be locked away. And you…. you are the one who got angry and stormed off like a fucking child leaving me alone with strangers, in a strange house, in a strange city. Fuck you, Cole, fuck all of you."

He stumbled as if I'd slapped him. "*That's* what's going through your head?"

"Not even half of it," I murmured. I moved to the bed, curling my legs up and dropping my head against my knees. I tried to fight the trembles wracking through my body but between the cold, rain and emotional riptide, I didn't have a chance. A blanket was tucked around my shoulders, and then Cole's weight beside me caused the bed to bounce.

"Then tell me the rest."

"No."

"Why?"

"Because the rest is just for me."

"When I found you, you fell into my arms with complete and utter blind trust. And in one stupid, childish fit of anger, I lost it all." He leaned to me, kissing my forehead with a slow deliberateness. "I'm so very sorry, Ariana."

He was leaving me. Leaving me alone, in the darkness, with absolutely nothing but my own terrorizing thoughts. "Please don't leave me alone again."

"I can have someone sit with you."

"I don't know any of these people. I know no one else on the whole damn planet."

"Ariana, we're both half drunk. I'm adrenaline fueled, and you're fragile…it's just not a smart situation."

"Cole," I whispered, "please don't make me beg."

He was beside me before I took a breath, tugging me into his lap, pressing my head into his chest and wrapping me safely in his arms. I'm not sure how long it took but my tears eventually ran dry, and the emotions raging in him finally calmed. In the quiet that followed, I became aware of how impossibly tight our bodies were pressed together. I felt something stir deep inside me, and I shifted in his lap, reaching my hand to caress his chest. I followed the curves of his muscles, memorizing the way they rippled under his shirt, the way I could feel his nipples hardening with my touch.

I reached to his caress his face, expecting to see a reproach but, instead, his eyes were alive with a dark, smoldering intensity. His fingers drifted across my cheek, bringing my lips to his. Our kisses were slow, exploring each other's mouths with an erotic jumble of both deep and shallow caresses.

His hands moved to my hips, lifting me and turning me to straddle him. It was only a tiny change in position, but it changed everything. I could feel his cock hard against me, and I let out a nervous breath. He tugged at my shirt, and I lifted it off, casting it aside as his mouth began to suckle my breast. As his hands wrapped around my back, pulling me tighter into his mouth, I knew I was fast losing any chance to say no. I knew I needed to stop him, to tell him that I'd never been this far with anyone, but with his mouth on me, it seemed too embarrassing even to consider.

His fingers slipped to my underwear, following the seam down to the center of my sex. His fingers fought inside the fabric, barely brushing against me, and he withdrew them, already slick with my juices. He let out a satisfied chuckle and rolled me to my back. He was taking off his pants, slipping my underwear from my legs and I knew it was my last chance to tell him. But I couldn't: the only thing more unbearable than the embarrassment would be if he stopped. I couldn't bear the thought of his touches ever ending.

He rolled on a condom and was back over me, rubbing my clit before pushing his fingers inside me. I spread my legs, wanting more, and he continued to thrust until I could hear my juices echoing in the room with his every plunge. His mouth was back on mine, his breath heavy and ragged as his cock edged against my opening. He entered me slow with a long, luxurious stroke as if he was savoring his first moment inside me. I winced as he began to swell, filling and stretching me, but his own moan covered my discomfort. His hands locked over my head, and he thrust again, deep and intense.

I let out the tiniest cry as my body tore open for him. Any hope I had that he wouldn't notice washed away when his every movement stopped, even his breathing. His hands flew to my face, cupping it firm to keep me from looking away. "Ariana-"

"No," I protested, "don't you dare stop this time. Not now."

"Look at me," he growled. When I finally lifted my eyes to his, I realized...he had had no intention of stopping. He lips dropped to mine, a long drawn kiss full of heat and promise. I could feel him inside me, gentle short pulses that matched my own anxious breaths. One hand released my head and moved to cup my ass. I tensed involuntarily, but his instructions were a tender caress against my throat. "Lift up, baby girl; it'll hurt less."

I let him lift me, tilting my body just slightly sideways and he was right...the sharpest of the pain went away. I tried to relax my body into his rhythm, the short, shallow pulses that had to be driving him mad. I closed my eyes, trying to memorize the feel of his cock, swollen and thick, pressing and filling every inch of me. Each tiny thrust stretched me to fit all of him as he seemed to grow even bigger inside me. His spasms came without warning, throbbing hard in my sex. He gave one last painful thrust, long and deep that he seemed unable to control and then locked himself there, deep within me, as he dropped his head onto the pillow beside mine. "Why," he groaned, "didn't you tell me?"

After several minutes of silence, he finally accepted that I wasn't going to answer. He shifted, his hand slipping to the rim of the condom. "This is going to sting. Just let out a long, deep breath, all right?"

He kissed my forehead as I nodded and then did as told. I felt him pull out, felt the raw sting of air against my battered flesh but, most vivid, was an overwhelming sudden and inexplicable feeling of loss at the absence of him.

"I'll be right back."

CHAPTER ELEVEN

Hm, so you are one of those women that get overrun by emotions after sex," Cole smiled and offered me a glass of whiskey. "I was going to offer wine, but you don't really seem the wine type."

"Not my favorite, no." I wiped my tears away and shuffled to sit against the headboard.

"Did I hurt you that much?"

"Discomfort, not pain, Cole. Pain has taken on a whole new meaning these last few days."

He frowned and opened his mouth to respond, but I stretched up and cut off his words with a slow, whiskey-scented kiss. I gave him a half smile and tapped the covers for him to join me. He crawled over me, kissing my lips as he moved passed, and tugged a tiny corner of the sheet over his bottom half.

"Suddenly shy?" I grinned.

"Trying not to entice you further. Your willpower is for shit," he chuckled. "So, tell me what thoughts brought tears before my manhood is totally shot to hell."

"I was just thinking of my mother. Wondering what her life was like in this family. She was just a child and yet she seemed to have a presence that made everyone stop and take notice. The loyalty that people had to her...it's unfathomable to me."

"You inspire it yourself if you haven't noticed. The men, they're drawn to you. You bring this lightness to such a dark world that they can't seem to ignore."

"Like a fucking magnet," I laughed.

"For their sakes, I hope not," he murmured, kissing my neck.

"What about you?" I asked, setting my glass down and turning to him. "Your thoughts seem to be somewhere else entirely as well."

He nodded, his hand slipping down my cheek. "I warned you how dangerous this could be."

"But I didn't listen."

He chuckled. "I'm not complaining about that part; I assure you. I just worry you don't understand the consequences."

"Is Cole Serrano, the reckless one, really lecturing me about consequences?"

"No, just feeling I have an unfair advantage."

"Men," I laughed, "usually do."

"Ariana, your father, will want to kill me for this, and in this life, this world, he certainly has that right."

"I won't let him."

"Such a spitfire," he chuckled. "You've not even met him."

"Do you doubt I'll protect you from my father?"

"I have no doubt you'll try," he murmured, his lips tracing down my bare shoulder.

"He took my mother when she was fourteen. I don't really think he has a right to judge."

"They were married."

My voice rose several octaves. "They were married? At fourteen? Are you serious?"

"It was a different world...and one he still clings to. The idea of his long lost daughter having sex will be hard enough for him to accept. Finding out it was with me, his problem child, and I took your virtue as well? That may be too much for even Franco to forgive."

"My virtue? Really?" I shook my head. "So medieval."

He gave me a quick kiss behind my ear, his voice soft. "Well, some traditions are worth the wait."

"You're the problem child?"

"You've no idea."

"Then you regret it?"

He shuffled me down on the bed, his hands cupping my face. "No, Ariana, not even for a second."

"You said touching me, being with me, was a one-time thing."

"I did say that," he admitted. "It was more of a rule for myself; an order issued that I knew I had no hope of following. I thought by saying it out loud it might make it more achievable. But, as you pointed out, I've been unable to keep my hands off you since the moment I found you in the Carolina house."

"I'm sorry for making you break your own rule."

"You are a true Catholic. Your guilt plagues you even as you lay naked in my arms." He smiled, his lips tracing along my collarbone. "But, you should have told me."

"I was afraid you'd say no."

"I probably would've worked a little harder to keep my urges in check, yes," he admitted. "But, Ariana, the moment I saw you writhing naked on that bed when you moaned by name without even realizing it, as you stroked every inch of your skin I knew I would take you. And then, on the sofa that morning...I had this desperate need to be inside you that, frankly, scared the hell out of me."

"Cole," I demanded before I lost my nerve, "teach me what you like."

He chuckled. "Is that an order, Ms. Valentine?"

I bit his ear and smiled. "Does it need to be?"

"It will be much more fun to teach you what you like," he murmured. "For example, right now, I know that despite how sore you must be, you still want me."

"Arrogant, aren't you?" I breathed but knew he was right. His light touches on my skin, the feathery kisses he placed strategically across my body - they were all making me dizzy.

His hand was heavy on my stomach, pressing hard as he moved it up my curves. "Look at your body flush, the heat rising off your skin." His hand cupped my breast, and I arched around him. His deep chuckle of satisfaction, of having proof of what his touches did to me, caused me to frown, but his lips were hot on my skin. His mouth took in my nipple, sucking and flicking until I let out a moan of pleasure. As he moved to the other with a harder bite, his hand slipped to lay on my pubic bone. "You have a fire growing here that's making you wet. And we both know how drenched you can be. It stings but you can't make it stop, can you?"

I whimpered, but he wouldn't accept that as a response. "Answer me, Ariana."

"No, I can't make it stop," I whispered. "I feel empty without you inside me."

He hesitated for the briefest second, and I was afraid I'd said something wrong. But after watching me, his movements picked back up where he left off. "You've given me a power over you. Whether you realize that or not."

"People lose their virginity all the time, Cole," I managed. "It's not that big of a deal."

"Really? Then why have you waited so very long to give it away?" I knew it wasn't a question I was expected to answer, and his touch between my thighs confirmed it. He was slow, careful to avoid my sex, but was purposefully spreading my juices to coat everything. He gave a low groan from somewhere deep within. "So fucking wet, Ariana. Christ."

He flopped onto his back, putting space between us. His cock was hard and tall again, and he made no move to cover it. I rolled to my side, my hand tracing down his chest. But he knew where I was heading and snatched my hand, kissing my palm.

"But no lessons today. Or tomorrow most likely. Your body will not thank me for that."

"There's no reason for you-"

"You get no release; I get no release. It's only fair." He kissed me on the forehead. "Give me a few minutes to recover and I'll draw you a bath."

I was drifting off, almost asleep, when he nudged me back awake and led me to the tub. Candles, bubbles, and a soft scent of ocean water filled the entire room. He gave me a sexy, cocky grin as he helped me step into the tub.

"I would've let you sleep, but I'm damn proud of myself for this."

I stretched out in the tub, my muscles relaxing as soon as I got under the bubbles. "Not usually the romantic type?"

"Not hardly. I don't imagine you to be one either. Despite the last name, Valentines aren't known for their romantic tendencies. Lust, not love, tends to be the motto."

"The irony of my life," I grinned.

"Speaking of, your mother used to give you a bath in this very tub."

"And you watched? Like you are now?" I laughed. "The more I learn about the Valentine clan, the kinkier it all becomes."

"Hey, I was seven and kept asking who broke off your peepee."

Peals of laughter rolled over me causing the water to ripple and shake in the tub. It took me several minutes to settle. When I did, his kiss was light on my forehead. "Your laugh," he murmured. "Best. Thing. Ever."

"Thank you," I whispered, "for helping me find it again."

He nodded but didn't reply and, instead, continued to thread his hands through the water. After several minutes, he finally exhaled.

"The men in this family…" he paused, searching for words to make me understand, "you've no idea how possessive we can be, Ariana. Your father has been looking for you for fifteen years. He will be an overbearing shit, afraid of losing you, for probably the next fifteen. And Marco. Whatever that is about-"

"I can't stand the sight of him, his touch, his smell-"

Cole calmed my shudder with a caress. "Nonetheless, he *is* possessive of you. You may not like it, but you damn sure need to be aware of it. I had a gun touching his head, and he still refused to let you go. It was foolish, but it also demonstrated an admirably deep commitment."

"Admirable?" I huffed. "I may never understand the mind of Italian men."

"You only need to understand one thing, Ariana: a man willing to die for something or someone is the most dangerous thing in the world."

"You fear him?"

"No, but I'm intelligent enough to recognize the danger he presents. I only wish I knew why. And before your temper flares, that wasn't an indictment of your memories. Your return is only one of many things that give me pause about Marco."

I nodded, accepting that as the only explanation I would be given. "Are you willing to die for something?"

"Ah, we get back to me," he chuckled. "I have risked everything for you. For your mother. In careless moments I've risked my life for your father before remembering who he is. I would die for the same men that are willing to die for me. So, yes, there are things I'm willing to die for."

"And are you possessive?"

He exhaled. "Unfortunately for you, yes. I can have quite the temper, and I'm already known as the reckless one."

"Are you possessive of everyone you've had sex with, then?"

"To some degree, yes, I suppose I am. But, I'll admit I was possessive of you and your mother long before tonight occurred."

"And now?" When he didn't answer right away, I turned to face him. "Cole?"

"I'm afraid the truth will scare you," he said with a broken smile. He leaned toward me, his hand dipping into the water and sliding along my outer thigh, tracing the outline of my body. "The truth? The truth is that knowing I am the only man who knows how impossibly wet you get, how fucking tight you are, that I am the only one you have ever begged to be inside you - it's the most erotic and powerful feeling I've ever experienced. And, yes, I'm possessive of that. Right now, strangling anyone who comes near you seems quite justified."

I felt myself twitch at the implication. "So, you're saying I'm stuck with you? That because you took my virginity I have no choice in the deal?"

"That infamous Valentine temper," he nuzzled my neck to get me to calm. "No, Ariana. It was your choice to give me that; it's your choice to let me have you again, or your choice to find someone else. I'm just saying it's now my job to make sure you always choose me."

"Good answer," I grinned and stretched up to kiss him, splashing water over the tub.

He laughed and pushed me back into the water. "Come on, your water's getting cold." He grabbed the shampoo bottle and squirted some onto my head. "I'll grab you another towel."

I sunk under the water, trying to rinse out the shampoo, when it hit me full force with no warning: fingers tight around my throat; heavy hands holding me underwater; my body thrashing; my lungs burning as the air was replaced with water; my mind slowly fading to black.

I was wrenched from the tub, water splashing everywhere. Strong hands bent me over, holding me steady as my body coughed and convulsed to get the water out of my lungs. A towel was pressed against me, and I skittered away, slipping on the wet floor. "Ariana, it's me. Look at me."

Cole. I nodded and moved back to his side. He dried me off fast then scooped me up and took me back to bed, tucking the covers around me as I continued to shiver. It took several minutes before I could even feel the calming strokes on my head.

"Better?"

I nodded, coughing again but able to manage a partial smile.

"That," he guessed, "is the half you keep for yourself."

"It's not-" I tried but started coughing again.

"I'm not going anywhere, Ariana. It can wait a few minutes," he said, kissing my forehead. "I'll call for some hot tea."

"Sweats," I murmured. "I asked Bridge-"

"I'll find them."

Even after I was snuggled into my sweats and tank top, Cole was still fussing over me. The tea had helped settle my mind, but my silence seemed only to agitate him more. When he finally sank down on the bed in front of me and touched my leg to get my attention, he seemed to have reached some decision.

"I'm man enough to admit that scared the shit of me, Ariana."

"Me too," I agreed.

"I know you believe I will judge you, and I don't know how to fix that. But if you won't talk to me, we have to find another solution because these things are killing you inside, baby girl. It's like a little piece of you disappears every time."

"My mom taught me to tell no one anything."

"And she was right. It kept you safe for a very long time but, Ariana, you are in a different world now, and we *will* keep you safe. It kills me that you trust me enough to share my bed but not enough to-"

"Please," I squeezed his arm to stop him. "I'm not that clever, I swear. Or even emotionally stable enough to think that clearly. The memories don't come complete. It's flashes. And you may know every single person who appears in them, but I don't, Cole. They are strangers on the street to me. I can't tell you anything more than a man did this or a man did that. Which is useless to both of us. It'll make you furious and make me a basket case all over again."

"That's it?" he tipped my head up to look at me. "Promise me, Ariana."

"Yes. This one...I could feel the water, smell and taste it, feel the fingers tightening around my throat and how my lungs burned. It was horribly graphic but, I saw no faces at all."

"How do you even face the fucking day, baby girl? I've faced hell before, but I can't imagine having to relive it like it's brand new over and over again without even a second of warning."

Knowing it would upset him, I lowered my voice. "Before now, it wasn't-"

"This bad," he said, and I could feel him take in a shuddering breath to calm himself. He put my teacup aside and pulled me to lay against his chest. "They're coming even more often, aren't they?"

I nodded but otherwise didn't respond as I tried to let his caresses calm my raging emotions.

He was quiet, and I knew he was trying to remember each one since he'd found me. "They come when you're relaxed, I've noticed. Like you mentioned - never when your mind's focused or intent on something. Twice when Valentine was in your system, drinking with me at the beach, and now this. Any others?"

"Please stop analyzing me."

"I'm trying to help, Ariana. To see if there's a common trigger we can avoid. Nothing more."

"Yes, there have been others," I admitted. "And yes, they were while I was alone or things were quiet."

His head dropped to my shoulder. "That's why you were so desperate about not being left alone or with strangers. I am such a fucking jackass to have not seen that."

"If you say I was childish-"

"No, it was responsible. This one almost drowned you." He hugged me tighter into his chest. "You told me before that they are always violent, but this was more than that. This was lethal, Ariana. Have you had others like that?"

A shiver rolled up my spine, and he brushed it back down. "That's a yes, then. Ariana," he murmured, "exactly how bad do these memories get?"

"The one earlier-"

"You mean in the tub, just now."

"No, before that. When the house emptied after dinner."

He checked his watch, his brows furrowing together. "You've had two? That close together?"

I nodded and tightened my fingers in his to try and stay focused on the present.

"The rain," he realized. "That's why you were out in the rain for all those hours."

"The sound of the storm lashing against the roof," I whispered. "It was the only thing that made it tolerable. Please tell Charlie I'm so very sorry. I didn't know-"

"You have the compassion of your mother, Ariana, but I personally don't give a damn if Charlie caught pneumonia."

"Cole!" A sharp knock caused us both to jump. "Wake up, brother."

"It's open, Tony."

"It's open?" I hissed.

Cole nuzzled my neck as Al and Tony strode in. "You are the daughter of Franco Valentine. No one, not even the old man himself, would enter your bedroom unannounced."

"Speaking of the old man," Al said, "he's waiting for you downstairs."

Cole made no move to leave. "He's early...as usual."

"And he knows you've been frolicking with his daughter."

"Frolicking?" I laughed. "Tony, did you really just say frolicking?"

"I told him he needed to tone down his language since there's a new lady of the house," Al offered.

"I imagine everyone in a five block radius is about to hear much more colorful language from both me and Franco," Cole grumbled.

"Well, he's waiting and getting angrier by the second. The families have started arriving and Franco's brought in the expanded security detail."

"Awesome," I mumbled, "more fucking people."

"Frolicking," Tony corrected.

Cole sighed. "Let me get dressed and I'll be down. Make sure there's coffee going for Ariana."

"Already done," Al said, winking at me as they left.

Cole tugged on a shirt and apparently that was as formal as he intended to get. He didn't even bother to reach for his shoes. I sighed and then began a search for something more suitable than sweatpants to finally meet my father.

"Don't take too long, okay?"

"Afraid to be alone with him?" I chuckled.

"I just don't want you up here alone in the quiet," he said, kissing my head.

I snorted. "I won't...dally."

"Dally and frolicking. What the hell have you done to this household?" he laughed but paused at my side. "Ariana, I need you to promise me something. I do have a temper, and it can sometimes be blinding. Franco's presence will draw it out even more often. I get distracted by work and trying to keep track of the thousands of backhanded dealings that are constantly swirling in this world. If you need me, and I don't see it, then make me see. Slap me, throw something at me, whatever it takes."

"You have so many more important-"

"Nothing," he promised, "is more important."

CHAPTER TWELVE

I took a tentative step onto the stairwell and the raging voices assaulted my ears. Cole and my father were somewhere and, from the sound of it, they were ready to kill each other. I inhaled a deep breath, readying myself for battle against the only two people I had left in the world. At the foot of the stairs I listened to gain some direction but, when I tried to turn the corner, I was met with a wall of men.

"Ms. Valentine." They all nodded in close unison, and I could only shake my head and the idiocy of it. Cole and my father sounded near blows, and they were standing by just letting it happen.

"It's probably best if you go back upstairs," Al said, stepping out of the opposite room with Tony. They each had a mug of coffee in their hand and looked completely unconcerned. That emboldened me, and I realized that, while the topic may be new, their fighting was apparently a routine dance to the men of the house.

"How bad is it?"

"It's escalating," Al frowned. "Cole's not his usual rational self."

"Wonder why that is," Tony chuckled and offered me the mug in his hand.

"And my father?"

"Totally unreasonable at this stage."

"Well, Cole could've eased that if he'd bothered to button his damn jeans before coming down. Reckless little shit."

I smiled in spite of the situation and then took a long draft of the coffee before handing it back. I straightened, exhaled a heavy breath, and then turned to face the testosterone wall. I steadied my voice as much as possible. "Move."

"Ms. Valentine-" a dozen voices spoke together.

"Get out of my way or I will have them," I nodded back to Al and Tony, "make you get out of my way."

I had no idea if it was true - they could have their own instructions to keep me away - but I was damn sure going to try.

I could feel them take a step up, closing in behind me. Tony's voice, normally so light and carefree, was a lethal hiss that made me understand why Cole had him at his side. "Give 'em hell, spitfire."

"You heard her," Al said, softer but equally as threatening.

They didn't need to repeat themselves, and the men moved aside. I braced myself before sliding open the silent door and stepping in, but I needn't have worried about being noticed. They were on the opposite side of the room, inches apart and throwing harsh words back and forth.

"I've loved her since the day she was born, Franco, just like you."

"That is not what I'm talking about, and you fucking well know it!"

"And I did not, as you so crassly put it, shove my dick in your daughter and then run off!"

"She was drugged, her mother just died, and you had no right-"

"I have whatever right she decides to give me. You've no idea what hell this has been on all of us. And you don't know because you were, once again, so fucking self-centered you couldn't even bother to come home!"

He staggered back, and I knew Cole had hit him somewhere deep. I intended to step forward right away, but the sight of my father made me hesitate. He was nothing like the fatherly figure I had imagined throughout my life. Instead, he was more the movie mafioso that little girls crushed on: tall and handsome with a sprinkling of silver hair threading through his black waves; muscled just like all the other Valentine men; dressed in some expensive suit that had to be hand tailored; and, perhaps most surprising of all, he looked as damned deadly as everyone had tried to warn me. It was easy to see why my mother loved him and just as easy to imagine why she'd ran away.

I exhaled and straightened which caused Cole's eyes to drift my direction. He jerked his head toward the door, telling me to leave but I stood firm. He closed his eyes, and I wasn't sure if he was cursing my stubbornness or trying to calm himself.

"Cole." When he didn't respond to my father's call, the voice dropped to a near-whisper. "Cole, I know she was like a mother to you. I know you loved her nearly as much as I. I can't imagine what it was like to witness her last moment, and I hate that I wasn't the one to have her in my arms at the end. It's a burden I never wanted you and certainly not Ariana to have. I despise everything about it and will live with that regret until my dying days. But," he took a settling breath, "you cannot love my daughter."

"Is that a house of Valentine rule someone forgot to mention?" I asked, making both men turn my way.

"Ariana-" my father was stepping toward me.

"Don't touch her," Cole's command stopped him in his tracks and my father whirled on him, fists already clenching. Before he could say anything, Cole was shaking his head. "It's not just you, she just has-"

"Issues," I provided. "Yes, I damn sure do."

"Ariana, we can discuss this later. Right now, having you home-"

"No. We'll discuss it now." I could see Cole cringe and his reminder about how dangerous my father could be, came storming back. But he wasn't the only one who could be reckless. "You seemed to think that my sex life was more important than visiting me - the daughter you haven't seen in almost two decades, the one whose mother bled to death in her arms, the one whose entire life was stripped away in seconds. So, if something is that fucking important, then we should probably discuss it now, don't you think?"

"You are as irrepressible as your mother."

"Yes," I admitted. "And you loved her for it."

His fierceness was gone, replaced with either exhaustion or resignation - I couldn't tell which. He sent me a tortured gaze and a slow shake of his head. "You know nothing of love, Ariana."

"I am a Valentine. We love fiercely and without rules. It is extraordinary, inexplicable, and, yet, somehow always..."

"Devastating," my father whispered the last word in unison with me. "How do you know that? Ariana, how can you possibly remember that?"

I bit my lip, faltering, but Cole was beside me, molding his body into mine. "Because she is your daughter, Franco. And she's finally home."

"I...you look so very much like her. It's breathtaking." My father shook his head, and I could see him trying to get his grief under control. Strength, I remembered, was the only thing he was allowed to show the world. He reached to touch my head but then drew his hand away. "I'll...just give me a minute, okay?"

He hurried out the door, and I couldn't help but feel crushed. The first time I meet him, the only parent I have left, and he runs away. Somewhere deep I understood that I looked too much like my mother. Probably almost identical to her the day she fled. But, the less forgiving part of me could only wonder: wasn't he supposed to be the fucking adult?

"That was the bravest thing I've ever seen," Cole murmured, his hand stroking along my spine. "Remind me never to doubt you again. Al? Tony?" He barely whispered their names, and they were at our side. "What time is it?"

"Almost dawn."

"Push back the meeting with Father Michael. Everyone in this house needs sleep before we kill each other."

"Will do."

"Franco isn't going to-"

"Then drug him," I interrupted. "Six hours, no more, no less."

"We cannot drug your father," Al hissed. "We have rules-"

"Your Valentine rules are shit and have done nothing but dismantle my entire life," I spat. Cole's fingers tightened at my waist in warning, and I let out a calming breath. "Give it to me and I'll do it."

"I'm not leaving you alone with him."

I gave him a half smile. "Was that even a consideration?"

"He's in the kitchen."

Tony was back in moments but before he could tell me what he drugs he was providing I waved him off. Cole's hand moved to the center of my back, directing me down the hall to the kitchen.

Cole's voice was a soft, but reprimanding, whisper. "We do have rules, Ariana, and he won't thank you for breaking them."

"Fine, Cole. Tell me your precious rules."

"We don't drug each other, especially without consent."

"Then you have a hell of a lot to answer for where I'm concerned," I huffed. "But it doesn't matter. I never intended to be subtle."

He opened his mouth to argue, but I pushed away and stepped into the kitchen. My father was sitting sideways at the table, a bottle of whiskey beside him and glass in his hand. At least I now knew where I got that predilection from.

I sank to my knees in front of him, clasping my hands in my lap. "I know I'm not the daughter you had hoped for. I am passionate and headstrong like my mother. But I can also be fierce, protective and loyal which I'm starting to learn comes from you. You don't know me, and I don't know you. That's something we can try and fix, or we can pretend it doesn't exist and let it haunt our every action. I'd rather we fix it."

Rather than touch me, he offered up his hand, waiting for me to accept it. When I did, he offered me a faint smile. "Your mother," he murmured, "was the best part of me."

"And me as well." I squeezed his hand. "But these men need you. My mother still needs you. And, stranger or not, you are my father, and I need you." He gave a single nod, and I motioned to Cole. He tucked the pills into my palm and then gave me some water. I stood up, pressing them both to my father. "So, please, will you get some rest for all of our sakes?"

He hesitated, his eyes drifting to Cole but then swallowed them without comment. He put the water glass aside, took the last swallow of his whiskey and then opened his arms to me. "Please, Ariana."

It took everything I had to step forward into his embrace. Once I was there, it felt impossible to leave. He was so warm, so strong and he smelled exactly like I'd always dreamed a father would...musky and minty with a tinge of whiskey and tobacco tying it all together. No matter what kind of man he was, he was my father.

I didn't realize my tears had started to fall, but my father's hands were soft on my face, wiping them away. "Cole, see Ariana to her room, please."

Cole's hands were on me again, directing me up the stairs and back to my room but, my head was so overwrought, that I missed the entire journey. Once behind closed doors, his arms enveloped me.

"All right?"

I nodded. "I'll be fine. That was just a hell of a lot more emotional than I expected."

"No one could prepare themselves for what you've been through or what you're going through now. Cut yourself some slack, okay?"

He led me to the bed, tucking me back under the covers. "You know, in all the time I've known him, I've never known Franco to take a single drug. Not even at times, like tonight, when he desperately needed it. What you did for him, for us, I don't think you've any idea the gratitude and respect that's going to come from that."

"I drugged my father, Cole. Please don't make it into some Valentine code of honor thing. I really can't handle that type of pressure right now."

"Just giving you fair warning."

"For chrissakes, please tell me there won't be more flowers."

He chuckled and kissed my forehead. "I'll see to it. You try and rest. I'm going to check on your father. I'll have Tony and Al right outside, but it'll just be a couple of minutes."

"You two were ready to kill each other," I protested.

"He's said his peace, made his position clear to me and I've made mine."

"So a stalemate."

"No," he laughed, "it's never that simple with Franco. He'll keep trying to get me away from you but the next time he argues; it will be with you."

"Awesome."

He laughed. "I'll be right back."

"But-"

"No one else will go check on him, Ariana, and don't forget he is my family too. Just like you, he's been through hell this week, and I'm sure he'd like a familiar face. Even if it's mine."

CHAPTER THIRTEEN

What the hell happened?"

"She just had a nightmare. Scared the shit out of us but, we're good. Aren't we, kid?"

I nodded but couldn't bring myself to look Cole's direction. I knew he would be checking his watch, surveying my every twitch and inhalation.

"Franco's out. Lock down the house and then put all the men on rotating shifts. I want everyone logging sleep and have meals brought in. All the house - well rested and well fed, no exceptions."

"Yes, sir." Tony ruffled my hair as he strode past and out the door.

Cole was beside me in two long strides. When he reached for me, I batted his touch away.

"Ariana-"

"Why did you lie to me? All of you?"

"What are you talking about?"

"Every one of you. Since the moment you've found me. Has every single thing been a lie?"

"I know you're upset-"

"Don't patronize me!"

"Then don't call me a fucking liar!" he roared. But just as fast as his temper flared, it vaporized, and he had his hands on my knees. "Ariana, look at me. Let's start over. Tell me what you've remembered."

"I saw them, Cole. Valentine men at my 16th birthday party. Laughing, joking, having a fabulous time with my mother."

"No-"

"I saw them! I saw the Valentine brands on their arms. You told me she'd fled. That she'd had no contact in fifteen years!"

"Not possible-" he mumbled, sinking onto the bed beside me. "It's just not."

"My mother stayed in contact this whole time. But you've sat here and lied to me from the moment I met you."

He locked my face between his hands, and it was impossible to doubt his sincerity. "Ariana, I did not lie."

"Then tell me something, Cole. Explain something, anything, to me instead of treating me like a fucking child that needs her hand held."

He nodded, but it took him several minutes to begin. "I was eleven when you and Teresa left. Your father, for what it's worth, tried to be what he envisioned a father should be. By the time I was fifteen he had no idea what to do with me, so I was inducted into the family."

"What does that even mean?"

"It means I developed a drug of my choosing, administered it to a person your father selected and then watched him die." His eyes were harsh on mine, refusing to look away, and I threaded my fingers through his. "I was never the best chemist. It took days as he slowly bled out and I had to sit through every agonizing second of it."

"That's why you are so careful now," I whispered. "So fanatical about the recipes and their side effects."

"I watched, I learned, and by the time I was twenty I'd proven myself invaluable to Franco. That's when he tasked me with finding you and Teresa...entrusted me with what I saw as the most personal of missions. Ariana, I've searched for six years. An absolutely meticulous search and yet I never even once came close." He turned to face me again, his eyes dark and intense. "I'm not lying. If men from the house of Valentine were in contact with your mother, I had no knowledge of it. And that contact was covered up by someone much, much more powerful than me."

"My father," I whispered.

"You don't know that. I don't know that."

"Then who else?"

"I don't know that either. But I do know that facts, rather than quick assumptions, are what will eventually help us find out."

He shifted, leaning against the headboard and then opened his arms. I climbed inside, curling my body against his and resting my head on his chest. His breaths were quiet, his heartbeat steady and I let his calm strength envelope me.

"He looked so broken every time my mother was mentioned."

"He was; he is" Cole assured me. "His love for her was indescribable. It was the love of legends, of fairy tales."

I turned, adjusting my legs to straddle him. His hands locked on my hips, pressing me tighter against him. That he wanted me, closer made a warm smolder start to rise somewhere deep inside.

I began undoing the buttons of his shirt, one by one. "But?"

"But, earlier, when he talked of burdens, your father-"

"Knew I was in the room when he gave his soul-stirring speech about regrets. I know, Cole. How many times will it take for you to believe me when I say I'm not a complete idiot?"

Rather than answer, his eyes narrowed on me. They followed my every move: each kiss against his bare chest; each stroke of my tongue along the ridges of his muscles; and each brush of my fingertips against the front of his jeans.

"Are you trying to seduce me?"

"Is it working?"

"Of course," he grumbled. He shifted me inches off his growing erection, tugging the button fly of his jeans wider open. His cock edged out, already thick and rigid. That I could make him so hard, so easily, made an irrational confidence swell within me. Cupping his hand over mine, he curled my fingers around his swollen shaft and began a slow, steady rhythm. When I had the pace and pressure he wanted, he let my hand go, and leaned back with a sigh of contentment. He sat in silence for a few minutes, watching me stroke him, and then the touched the tips of his fingers to my knee.

"I do love you, Ariana."

"You've known me for a week."

"I've known you all your life," he corrected. "You've only known *me* for a week. And love has no rules to you Valentines. What was it? Fierce, inexplicable, extraordinary..."

"Devastating, Cole. The important one."

"Then I suppose it's a good thing that both of us are too reckless to give a damn about consequences, hm?" A single finger touched my temple and traced down over my lips. It continued a trail: first to one nipple, then the other, and then danced across my navel before zig-zagging down to outline the shape of my thighs. "Speaking of reckless," he murmured, "how are you faring?"

"You know damn well how I'm faring," I grumbled.

And it was true. He was too observant to have missed the shallowing of my breath, my nipples growing hard and erect against the heather cotton of my shirt, and the way I had been subtly rocking myself against his leg as I stroked him.

"You have a curiously strong sexual appetite. Is that my influence or are you using me to ignore all the other emotions twirling out of control in your head?"

"Both. Always both."

"At least you're honest about it," he laughed. "In the future, feel free to use me to your heart's content. But, for now," he took my hand from his crotch and kissed my palm, "we are under strict orders to sleep."

"Aren't you the one who ordered us all to sleep?"

"No, baby girl," he chuckled, "that was you. I'd happily break my own rules any day, but yours are an entirely different matter."

"Remind me never to do that again," I grumbled but moved to lay beside him, curling my back into his chest and squeezing him so tight I could barely breathe. "I feel like-"

He shifted her bodies closer, molding them together where I could still feel his cock long and hard against my flesh. He rested his mouth at my throat. "What?"

"I feel like no matter how close you are; it's never close enough."

"Empty," he murmured. "That's what you said. You felt empty without me inside you."

"And it scared you," I said, finally able to understand the emotion on his face that I'd been unable to define.

"Yes," he admitted, "when I always thought myself fearless." His touch was soft against my hair, following a path from the tip of my head, down my shoulders and over my arm to rest at his favorite spot on my hip. "When you and Teresa left, it felt like my world was torn apart. I felt alone, adrift and..."

"Empty,' I whispered.

"Yes. I never want you to experience that, Ariana. It leaves a mark on your soul that isn't easily forgotten." He nudged me. "Hey, look at me."

I rolled around in his arms; our noses inches from each other. His voice was a quiet hum. "Have they ever been this bad? This close together? And don't lie."

I shook my head.

"Do you think it's here? If it's too much, if I'm too much, or we are too fast, too..."

"No," I cut him off with a soft kiss. "It may be the stress or it may be its just time for me to know them. Maybe it's because I've been thrown into a past I never knew existed. I don't have the answers. I wish I did. But I do know you are the only thing right now that *doesn't* give me nightmares."

"This one was different. You weren't-"

"A child, I know." There were probably a million more things I needed to say, but I just couldn't bring myself to vocalize it. It didn't matter - he already knew. If I remembered things from such a recent time, there was no telling what else my mother had hidden away in my brain.

"I know you'll tell me about your memories when you're ready. And I don't want to bring on another-"

"Cole, please just ask me whatever it is."

"The Valentine men, from your party - could you see their faces this time?"

"Yes."

A pained look caused the muscles in his jaw to twitch, but it was gone as soon as it appeared. No doubt wishing I could name them for him. "Were either Al or Tony there?"

"You doubt them?"

"I doubt everyone, Ariana," he murmured, "and that doubt is what's going to keep the two of us alive."

I stretched up, kissing his neck and placing my hand against his cheek. "No, neither of them."

His returned my kiss, drifting his lips across mine. "Thank you."

CHAPTER FOURTEEN

Although I tried exceptionally hard to get out of the meeting at the church, neither Franco or Cole would hear of it. Instead, after taking ten minutes for them to down sandwiches, they were ushering me down the street the few blocks to the church. Franco was grousing about security, demanding cars be readied for the funeral mass, and Cole was nodding in silent accommodation. Apparently, the various families already had representatives at the church, and the men would be meeting to discuss seating, safety, and who was actually deemed worthy of admission to my mother's funeral. They acted like it was a freaking carnival show or wedding and my irritation continued to grow with each step closer.

As soon as we entered the building, we were surrounded by a cluster of Valentine men. Franco squeezed my hand and offered a reassuring smile. "The men aren't much for personal space. They'll have to learn that about you."

His words caused the circle to loosen, but I still could've reached out and touched each of them. I swallowed a shuddering breath, trying to find Cole in the madness but everyone looked the same from my rather short viewpoint.

"Want an arm, spitfire?"

Tony's quiet voice beside me made me smile, and I nodded, tucking my arm into his.

"He had to do a sweep of the hall," Al explained from my other side. "It's already been done, but Franco wanted Cole specifically to do another."

I opened my mouth to question his choice of words just as I was yanked into a massive embrace. I was choking before Tony had me free. He gave me an apologetic shrug. "I would've slugged him for you, but I think there's a special place in hell for people that do that. Ariana, meet Father Michael."

He was ancient but spry, maybe? I wasn't even quite sure how to describe the man before me. He seemed perfectly at ease among the Valentine men, and he kept reaching out to touch my head like I was some gift.

"So much like Teresa," he whispered.

It took everything I had not to snap at him.

"I married them, did you know? And baptized you and Cole. Most of the men here actually."

"Baptizing the devil's army," I groused, low under my breath and Tony fell into a coughing fit as he tried to cover his laughter.

"Sorry, Father. The incense, just-" Tony had to step away fast to get himself under control.

"Will you be taking confession, Ariana? It's been so long since we talked."

"Confessionals are closed," my father spat.

"It's tradition, Franco," Father Michael reprimanded. "And your men, I'm sure, could use a little time in the confessional."

I can't imagine there were many people my father tolerated insolence from, but apparently, Father Michael was one of them. They were arguing in polite terms when a familiar shadow finally appeared beside me.

Cole's warm touch was on my lower back; his voice low at my ear. "Do you have things to confess, Ariana?"

"To a priest on the Valentine payroll? I think not."

"So very clever." He gave me a soft stroke. "We're set up in the banquet hall to the right, but there will be men on patrol everywhere. Do you want me to have Al and Tony-"

I glanced to the open doorway where I could see the long table already encircled by men. None of them looked happy which made me wonder how safe Cole and my father were even in this church. "No, it's fine. Take them with you."

"You certain?"

I sent him a glare, and he raised his hands. "Okay."

He started stepping away, but I grabbed his coat jacket. "Do you have a rosary?"

"Not on me but I can get you one."

"Here," my father tugged one of his pockets. "It was your mother's."

It wasn't some meaningful exchange I might have hoped for. In fact, it seemed to barely register in my father's conscious, and he was already stalking toward the gathering up ahead. So I simply nodded. "Gee, thanks, Dad."

Cole chuckled at my sarcasm then gave me a soft tap on the hip. "If you need me-"

"I know where to find you. It's a church not the Vatican museum, Cole."

"So feisty today," he murmured. "Did you skip your coffee this morning?"

I *was* testy, but I had no real excuse for it. We were in the church where my mother's memorial service would be held, her ashes were even here somewhere, and there were dozens of cartel men everywhere, but none of that even seemed relevant. Instead, there was something in the pit of my stomach nagging away with a nervous underpinning. Taking a seat in the back, I fingered the rosary, hoping for some sense of calm. I hadn't actually prayed it in years, but there were some things a cradle Catholic could never forget. I let my hands caress the cranberry red beads that had been worn smooth after years of use. Finally, there was something familiar in all the chaos of my life. I could picture my mom holding it, pressing the bronze cross to her lips, her pinky finger always locked on the dove charm that was so fascinating to me as a child.

I had been reciting the prayers for over an hour when angry words filtered from the men's table at the front of the church. Franco was on his feet, Cole beside him and other Valentine men encircling them. Men around the table, other families I presumed, were getting up as well. Many were in placating positions, but several looked ready to fight. I glanced around for Father Michael, but he had hidden himself away in the confessional and seemed in no hurry to come out. I closed my eyes, tightening my grip on the rosary in hopes of making it all just disappear. I envisioned my mom, on the beach, the rosary twisted onto her wrist and dangling from her palm. But, no, that wasn't right. It wasn't the red of her rosary...it was blood. My eyes fluttered open, staring at my own wrist and saw long scratches of blood. I tugged my sleeve down, sure I was just losing my mind, when the metal tink of a knife against my crucifix, made the memories all rush back. The screaming...the fighting...the grit of sand mixed with blood. It assaulted my senses just as streams of lightning coursed through my body. I curled instinctively, my body sliding off the pew and collapsing to the floor like a blanket of darkness engulfed me.

"Ariana."

I knew it was Father Michael's voice, but I couldn't place his location. I tried to move, but my body seemed just too heavy to cooperate. I closed my eyes, trying to remember what the flashback had been about it. Men, I thought and then realized how idiotic that sounded...it was always about these damned Valentine men, wasn't it?

"Get Cole. Now."

No. Not Valentine men, this time, that was what had been different. Other men, from other families. And me. But not little me. I was a teen. They had found us, and we had run. But not before I slit his throat. "Not possible. Not possible. Not possible."

"Ariana, look at me."

I tried to look but couldn't find anyone. It was so dark, so very dark. I felt my body shake, not a lot but enough to rattle off some of the darkness.

"Ariana." More urgent this time. "Tony!"

"Not possible. Not possible. Not possible."

"Where did that knife come from? Is that hers?"

"Hey, kid, can you look at me?"

I tried to smile but had no idea if it worked.

"Somebody get the knife and bag it."

"I'm going to touch you, okay? Just want to check you over. Alright?"

"Ariana."

Not possible. Not possible. Not possible.

"Tell us something here, Father."

"I came out of the confessional, and she seemed to be having a seizure. Her whole body-"

"Fast facts, Father, or I'll-"

"Take that gun away from him. Cole, either settle down or get the hell out."

"Little shocks all over her body, and then she couldn't seem to hear anything, and then blacked out for a bit but came to and couldn't see anyone."

"Much better, Father, thank you."

"TMS," I mumbled.

"Will everyone just shut the hell up?" Tony's booming voice made my whole body quiver, but everything did go quiet. "Tell me again, kiddo."

"You can hear me?" I shook my head. I thought I'd said that in my head.

"Barely because of these stupid shitheads. Sorry, Father."

"Understood. The Lord forgives in times of-"

"That didn't mean you could talk."

"Yes, Cole."

"TMS," I repeated.

"She's talking nonsense-"

"If everyone doesn't shut up-"

"Childish. You men are so childish."

"Yeah, kiddo they are. Tell me one more time, okay? Cole has a gun to their head, so they are gonna be quiet for you this time."

I tried to think of something that Tony would understand. "TMS. Marine Corps. PTSD. Walter Reed."

I could feel Tony's hot breath on me as he exhaled. "Good job, kid. Father, can we move her to a room somewhere? Got a sofa or something? She's gonna be fine, but we need her away from anything metal."

"Yes, of course. Follow me."

"Cole, your watch!"

And then everything went pleasantly black again. It seemed much shorter this time, though I had no reference. I was jostled for a little bit and then was finally left untouched. A warm weight was dropped on me, and I could feel Cole's hand brushing against my hair. I was in his lap, I knew how it felt to be here, how his thigh curved against the shape of my neck. But maybe that wasn't even real either. Maybe all of that was actually the dream.

Not possible. Not possible. Not possible.

"What part of no metal didn't you understand?"

"Fuck you."

"Don't let Father Michael hear you say that."

"So-"

"Transcranial magnetic stimulation. You told her I was ex-military?"

"Yes, in passing."

"Damn smart of her to pick up on that to clue me in. I would've still been going through an alphabet of street drugs. TMS is in trials to treat military patients with PTSD. Only a couple of hospitals have permission to use the technology since it's so experimental. It delivers-"

"Tony, for chrissakes-"

"It's a taser specifically for brain function."

"Who?"

"Goretti maybe. They went through an electronics phase."

"Or Bianchi. They generally take the clean route."

"It's too bold. It's as if someone *wants* to start a war."

"Yeah, at Ariana's expense."

"Cole, she's not even safe in a damn church."

"Not possible. Not possible. Not possible."

"Welcome back," Cole's soft voice was next to me. "It is possible because it happened but I can damn sure guarantee-"

"Cole, that's not what she's talking about. She's been repeating that for a while. Father Michael heard it before she blacked out the first time."

"Al. Always so calm and reasonable. No matter what."

"Yes, yes he is."

"Wait, you can hear me?" I opened my eyes and had to blink back from the influx of colors.

"Get the lights off, turn on those lamps. Sorry, kid, didn't think about that."

I waited until the clicking noises stopped and then tried again. It took several minutes for the shapes to turn into shadows and then actual people. I offered a half smile to the trio. "My heroes."

"Heroes would've prevented this in this first place."

"Cole, stop being such an ass," I coughed. "Can I have some water?"

One of them helped me shuffle to sitting as a plastic bottle, already opened, was placed in my hand. I took a quick drink, making certain it wasn't going to revolt, and then drank down most of the bottle. "For the record, I'm against TMS as a treatment for any fucking ailment on the planet. Just so you know."

"Duly noted."

Cole's voice made me feel all warm and fuzzy, and I smiled...until he spoke again.

"So what's not possible?"

The memory came back instantly and in its entirety. Brilliant, vivid and much, much too real. My body's reaction was only a split second behind the one in my head.

"Ariana, look at me." His hands were clenching my shoulders, pinning me to his lap, and we were both doused in water. "Breathe, baby girl, and look at me."

"Sorry. I'm so sorry." I glanced to Tony and Al who were observing in silence. "Sorry."

"Wait until you see me really drunk and then tell me if you have something to apologize for."

The soft laughter was warming, and I could feel the tension in my body starting to release.

"Better," Cole whispered. "Still not good, but better."

I hadn't even realized he was checking me again but, when I glanced down, his fingers were wrapped around my wrist.

"Any lasting effects from TMS?"

Tony shrugged. "Depends on what the hell that was."

"Please don't patronize me. I know he tells you two everything."

"Everything about *business*, Ariana," Cole corrected. His fingers drifted light across my cheek. "I would never tell them something so personal without your permission."

"But-"

"Ariana, it's always your choice."

I nodded and, buying time, began tugging at my wet clothes.

"I'll find you a towel."

"And coffee. I bet you're ready for some coffee."

It was sweet. These two men, killers both of them, and they were making up excuses to leave and give me privacy. "I'll accept both, but could you come back? I think it might help if I tell you some things."

"You got it, kid."

"Are you sure?" Cole asked as soon as they were gone.

"I'm sure they need to know I could black out on them at any second. Anything more, no, I'm not."

"Fair enough. The rate they're occurring-"

It was an observation, not a question, but I replied anyway. "I know."

"This one seemed-"

"The worst," I whispered. "Cole, the worst it's ever been."

"You remember all of it, the entire memory, this time, don't you?"

I nodded, afraid of blacking out again if I thought too much about it. His hand slipped under my shirt, resting along my ribs, and he began the soothing pattern of strokes that calmed me every time.

"You're not alone anymore, Ariana, and you have armies to protect you now."

"Those armies, Cole, are what frighten me most."

He opened his mouth to demand clarification, but Tony and Al were back with blessed timing. I sat up and accepted the towel, drying myself off as much as possible before handing it off for Cole to do the same. Then I wrapped my hands around the steaming mug and inhaled the scent before taking a long drink.

"My brain," I offered, "is a little dysfunctional."

"That is *not* how we are going to start this conversation," Cole said, cutting me off. "She has no memories before she was five. She didn't know she was a Valentine and remembers nothing of her life before Teresa took her."

"Wait," Tony sat forward, tension etching through his shoulders. "Are you telling me, we pulled you out of a house, brought you to a strange place with guns and drugs around every corner, where you don't know a single fucking person? Cole, I know you can be a raging asshole, but you have got to be kidding me here."

Al's eyes were narrowing at Cole. "Ditto."

"Stop, please stop. It's not as if he had a choice, did he? Everyone was following their precious Valentine orders, and I was immediately drugged if you remember. It's not like he even knew until after I was already locked away in Atlantic City. Besides," I gave them a quick smile to try and relieve the tension, "I adapt well and it's not like I had anywhere else I could go."

"You, kid, are a hell of a lot more forgiving than I would be. To any of us." Tony sank back, still huffing. "Fucking monsters. We are fucking monsters."

"They *are* right, Ariana. If we'd known, everything would've been handled differently, but we weren't given that option. But, she's right as well. Franco's orders were explicit, and she was going to be brought back no matter what. Once I learned, I've done my best to make the transition easier, and she *is* amazingly adept at navigating everything that's been thrown at her."

"Does Franco know?"

"No, and I'd prefer he didn't."

Both men nodded their promise, but Al's curiosity got the better of him. "Can you tell us why you feel that way?"

"I've been getting flashbacks or visions; I don't even know what they are. I don't know if they're real or just imagin-" I trailed off. That wasn't true anymore. I *knew* the one tonight was real. I had no doubt in my mind.

Ever observant, Cole had noticed the tension wash over me. His hand was at my lower back, sitting forward to look at me. "Ariana?"

But I shook my head. "If they are all real, then my life as a Valentine was a really fucked up childhood."

"That sounds about right," Tony agreed.

"No," Cole cut off his humor. "These are things so dark, so violent, that it makes the world stop when they hit her."

There was something in his tone, some nonverbal communication I missed, that made Tony lean forward. "It's what was happening on the beach, after the club, wasn't it?"

I nodded.

"And you had them before you came here, didn't you?"

Al frowned. "Why would you think that?"

"You don't learn about experimental PTSD drugs in a textbook. You," he accused, "had been doing your research long before you ever came here."

"True," I admitted. "It's also true that they are coming more frequently and are more..." I trailed off, uncertain.

"Lethal," Cole supplied.

"I'm not going to ask what it was, but did you have one tonight? In the chapel?"

"Yes."

Cole's eyes turned to Al. "Why?"

"Tony was telling me about TMS while we waited for the coffee. I know nothing about it, but it makes sense to me that if she was having one when they hit her, it would've short-circuited everything."

"Great," I grumbled, "now my brain is actually fried instead of just dysfunctional."

"No," Tony laughed. "He means it might explain why this one was so much more realistic. They could continue to get more graphic as time wears on. That happens to vets a lot as memories come back. But, it could also just be a fluke, a one-time thing because of the way the device works."

"Let's hope for that one," I huffed. "So, there you go. Just in case I start freaking out on one of you, I figured you might should know. And keep your weapons away from me, that's probably an excellent move as well."

I had tried to make light, but the instant tautness that rocked through Cole's body made me re-think my words. I'd said something that set him off, put him on edge, but I couldn't define what it might have been. I chanced a look at him, and his eyes were an intense but unreadable dark brown.

"What's 28 seconds?"

"Hm?"

"You kept repeating 28 seconds," Al explained.

I looked to Cole for confirmation. He gave a slow nod, almost apologetic. "You say it all the time actually. When you were high on Valentine, when you're drinking, in your sleep, the moments you just sort of zone out...you chant it almost like a mantra."

I frowned, wondering what else I'd been stupid enough to say without realizing it.

"Never mind," Al whispered, "none of my business."

"It's not...I mean, it's fine," I said, offering him a half smile. "It's just...it's how long the video lasted. The one that let the families find us, got my mom killed, and-"

"Stopped your world spinning," Tony finished.

"I'm going to take her back to the house to get some rest. Make sure Franco doesn't get so distracted by guests that he forgets he has a family dinner engagement."

Tony was at my side before Cole could sweep us away. He reached out his hand, letting it hover above my head. When I nodded, he pulled my head down and gave me a hard kiss on the top of my head. "I'm sorry, Ariana...Ms. Valentine...what the hell ever. I wouldn't blame you for hating me forever, but I swear to you, I'll make it up to you no matter how many lives that takes."

He was away before I could even open my mouth to respond and Al took his place. His eyes dropped away, and I squeezed his arm. "I know, Al. Ditto, right?"

"Yeah. Ditto." He grinned, kissed my hand and was gone.

CHAPTER FIFTEEN

I thought we were going home."

"I need some air. Do you mind?"

I shook my head and stepped to walk beside him down the boardwalk. I glanced over my shoulder, the handful of men following behind us causing my nerves to twitch.

"You'll get used to them," he promised.

"Not likely."

He tugged off his tie and tucked it in his inner pocket. "Oh, here," he pulled out my mother's rosary from the pocket. "Found it in the pew."

"Thanks." I weaved the chain between my fingers, letting it slip back and forth against my thumb.

He nodded to it as he unbuttoned the first few buttons of his shirt and took a breath like he'd been suffocating. "It's a Valentine family heirloom. The beads, they are drusy agate, said to encourage trust and allow the holder to discern truth. Supposedly blessed by St. Valentine of Rome himself." He grinned. "You know, before his best friend the Emperor beheaded him for marrying people in secret to keep them out of the war."

"Lies, betrayal, deception, love and war. It sounds like modern Valentines are just keeping up a long-standing tradition, hm?"

Cole chuckled. "I hadn't thought of it that way but, yes, I suppose so."

"She never told me its history or anything, but she never went anywhere without it," I murmured, fingering the beads as we walked. "She carried it almost like a talisman. I never thought I'd see it again."

"Wait, what?" Cole stopped mid-stride. "You've seen Teresa with this? Recently?"

"Of course. Whoever saved it from the house-"

"Ariana, we took nothing from the house. You, your half empty duffel, and Teresa's body. That's it."

"No, this-"

"The house was in flames. I assure you, we didn't take the time to search it. I would not have *allowed* your father's men to search it."

"But-" I glanced at the rosary and then tucked it into my pocket as if I could protect it from his veiled accusations.

"When is the last time you remember seeing her with it? Not a guess, but are absolutely certain she had it in her hand?"

I frowned as I tried to think. I hadn't been attending regular Sunday mass with my mother for most of the summer, but I knew I'd seen her with it. I remembered the street lamps reflecting on the antique bronze as we had walked home barefoot from the church, our sandals swinging in our hands. "The Vigil of St. James."

"That's over a month ago."

"I'm sorry! I spent most Sundays on the beach."

"For chrissakes, I'm not judging your mass attendance, Ariana." He waved me up to the entrance gate of the pier.

I hesitated, frowning. "I'm not really up for carnival rides."

"The noise and chaos," he explained. "It should help keep those demons at bay despite what I intend to say."

I nodded, and he purchased the tickets. He waved for the guards to stay behind and led me through the gate.

"I promised you I wouldn't push, and while that's still not my intent, it may end up coming out that way."

I slipped my hand through his arm, trying to calm the flutter in my stomach. "You want to know about the memory from the chapel."

"I know you are convinced it was real. I know it was more graphic than any you've had so far. Considering that one almost drowned you, that has to be saying something. And, I know that you've never flinched when having guns around but you suddenly-"

"Knives, not guns," I corrected quietly. "I'm not nearly as clever as you think if you learned all that."

"Well, it took electric shock therapy for you to let things slip so I'd say you're still pretty damn good," he said. "But I do need to ask: if you think my men are in danger if you think they could be harmed...Ariana, they have a right to know."

"I wouldn't hurt them."

"On purpose. We all know that, but-"

"I killed someone before, Cole...before the Carolina house."

His steps did not even pause, his stride as strong and confident as always. "Taffy? Sour grape was always your favorite."

I nodded, knowing he was allowing me time to calm my nerves. He kept me attached to his side as he ordered from the stall. He unwrapped the first one for me, popping it in my mouth, and then led me to the railing. I could feel the sea spray coming in drifts that matched the waves, the cold droplets settling on my skin and making goosebumps rise to the surface. I started to open another taffy, but Cole stopped me, his fingers warm on my cheek. He leaned in and pressed his lips to mine. His kiss was gentle and unhurried, a mix of anticipation and longing that was almost indescribable in its depth.

"That," he whispered, "should've been our first kiss."

"Sour grape and sea salt on Steel Pier?"

"Yes," he smiled. "I've dreamed about it pretty much my whole life."

Reckless. Powerful. Intimidating. Deadly. And about the sweetest fucking man on the entire planet. I stretched up, kissing his jaw, and then tucked a taffy into his palm. He chuckled, popped it in his mouth and then tucked me close at his side as we turned to look back over the railing.

After several minutes of silence, he finally sighed. "Friend or foe?"

"Foe. No doubt."

"Then that's all I need to know."

"But-"

"I would love for you to share everything with me. I want you to trust me enough to do that. I want you to trust yourself enough to do that because, no matter how dark you think they are, you *are* a good person, Ariana. But, what I want and what I need are two very different things. You gave me the information that I need." He leaned sideways to give me a peck on my temple. "Anything more is all up to you."

"You weren't surprised."

"You are a Valentine," he reminded, smooth as silk.

"Well, it shocked the hell out of me."

"Very unfortunate word choice, Ariana."

His mischievous glint caused me to giggle which fast turned into a rolling fit of laughter. It was so insane, all of it, that I couldn't do anything but laugh. My eyes were watering from the laughter when he shifted to face me. Cupping my face in his hands, he thumbed away the laughing tears at the same moment they turned into something much darker.

"We were in California, having a cookout on the beach when they found us. Three men and they saw my mother, but they came for me first. I don't know why they came for me instead. My mother fought them, but we were losing. She pulled a knife from somewhere, no idea where, and stabbed one of them."

"Breathe, Ariana, I'm right here."

"The other, he got so angry. He started screaming and then my mother was screaming, and he was on top of her trying to strangle her. I took the knife and slit his throat. Cole, I *slit* a man's throat. It wasn't even something nice and clean like a gunshot or something."

I knew I had completely lost it. I was sobbing into his chest, his arms clasping me so tight his hands overlapped on my shoulders. "Not that that would excuse anything, I mean, but, Cole, I sliced a person open, and he choked to death on his own blood. Who does that? What kind of person am I-"

"You are the daughter of Franco and Teresa Valentine. You are fiercely loyal and protective. You are clever and compassionate, damn sexy and yes, a little bit broken. You are the girl who protected your mother when she needed you most. You are the woman that will see your father through, and you are," he whispered, "the absolute love of my life."

CHAPTER SIXTEEN

Tony and Al were waiting for us at the door as soon as we arrived. "Slight change of plans."

Cole groaned. "What does that mean?"

"Franco's cleared out the Knife & Fork for the family meal. It was apparently Ariana's favorite place?"

It was a question, but I didn't know the answer to it. As usual, though, Cole did.

"In the history of time, no toddler has ever loved Knife & Fork. I guess more people have been added to the guest list?"

"Yes. Still a private room for the family but the people who arrived for the memorial will be there as well. He's had Bridgett get formal attire for everyone and wants us all for a chat in about an hour. The security councils will meet pre-dawn tomorrow to finalize details for the service."

"Fine, fine, whatever." Cole glanced at the shopping and garment bags piled in the foyer. "Bring all that shit up."

I frowned at the packages and tried to grab a few, but Al laughed at me and gently pushed my hand away. "Us, not you."

I shoved a handful into Cole's arms and then took a few myself. "I may be new, but I'm not new enough to mistake you for a maid."

"Don't even say it, Tony," Cole grumbled with a smile. "Spitfire, I know. Hand me a few more."

They were all chuckling at me as I tromped up the stairwell, loaded down with a mass of bags.

"I'm gonna get a quick shower." Cole began stripping off his outerwear then held up his arm for me to remove his watch and cufflinks. I undid each, wiggling my eyebrows suggestively which earned me a cocky grin in return. My hand brushed across his Valentine mark before putting his watch aside. I turned to Tony, trying to shake off the sexual tension I could feel building.

"Do the other families brand people, too?"

"They mark each other, but everyone has their own way. Some use tattoos; some use knives, or I know the Gorettis, fucking lunatics that they are, shoot their people to leave the mark of a bullet wound."

Al stepped in, dropping another shopping bag on the bed. "Why do you ask?"

"Just curious."

"Cole," Tony called, "do you get that same tingly feeling on the back of your neck whenever your girl here says those words?"

"It is a little terrifying, isn't it?" Cole chuckled as he began unbuttoning his shirt.

"I would say have fun, but you've only got an hour so..." Tony shrugged, "do with it what you will."

"Out, Tony."

He gave a mock salute followed by a tiny wink. "Yes, ma'am."

I riffled through a few of the garment bags. I have to admit either my father or Bridgett had exceptionally good taste: top end dresses in a style that was classy but still a little sexy. Unfortunately, every single one was sleeveless.

"Nothing to your liking?" Cole asked, slinking up behind me. "You've never struck me as the high maintenance type."

"I can't wear these," I admitted. "They're beautiful but, could we find something with a little less skin showing, maybe?"

"I rather like your skin showing," he said, nuzzling my neck. "But, yes. If you want to be demure tonight, then I'll have Bridgett find a shawl or jacket or something for you."

"Thanks." I turned in his arms, my lips doing a slow dance across his chest. Each defined muscle, each curve of skin...I wanted to memorize them all.

"28 seconds..."

I buried my teeth into his skin to cut him off. "I think I've had enough soul searching conversations already today." He made no comment and had no protest when I began undoing his fly, one button at a time. He was impossibly hard already, his cock fully erect and standing out long from his body. I shifted down to my knees, kissing each defined edge of his abs on my way down. "How about, instead, we make a much better memory."

"Ariana-"

I bent forward, letting my tongue run up one side of his shaft and then the other. I circled the tip, uncertain of the pressure, and then traced the cleft that led to his opening. He gave a violent shudder, and I stopped, eying him with uncertainty.

"Good thing," he mumbled. "Good thing."

I laughed and then wet him all over again before taking a gentle suck of the tip. His hands moved to the back of my head, tangling in my hair, and he pulled my mouth to cover his shaft. "Circle your tongue."

As he continued to slide in and out of my mouth, I swirled my tongue around him, causing a guttural moan to build somewhere deep within him. "Flick me along...christ, yes, just like that." I let my fingernails trace light against the stubble of his crotch, wrapping down to cup his tightening balls. "Faster, baby girl, take me faster." I began moving my mouth, bouncing up and down against his cock.

His moans became lower, desperate, and I knew he almost there. I could feel my own wetness sliding down my thighs, and I reached one hand down to stroke myself as I continued to suck him off. His liquids started to trickle into my mouth just as spasms rocked my own body. I lurched my hands up to grip his ass, desperate to have him deep inside me. I took him down my throat, and a string of curse words came just as he exploded in my mouth, a fountain of salty semen nearly choking me.

"Sorry, sorry," he chastised himself and readjusted both of us. "I meant to pull out, but you got me there so fucking fast...no warning. So sorry, Ariana. You can spit, it's okay. Most women don't like-"

I swallowed him down, silencing his apologies, and then returned my mouth to his cock, sliding my tongue against the last of his pulses. When he was finally soft and clean, I slid up his body to kiss him hard on the lips. "I am not most women, and I can't imagine wasting a single part of you."

His kiss was still intense; his breathing ragged, but his voice held a tranquil passion. "The more I learn of you, each minute I spend with you is somehow more breathtaking and astonishing than the last."

"Devastating, Cole. Don't forget devastating."

"I'm willing to risk it," he chuckled and wrapped his arms around my waist. "Does the idea of falling in love with me terrify you that much?"

"Yes."

He hadn't expected an honest answer, and he tilted his head back to survey me. "Why?"

"Because I lose everyone I love, Cole."

"Stop worrying so much, Ariana, and let yourself be happy. Otherwise, everything else is pointless." He gave me a sweet, tender kiss and then tugged at my arm. "Come on, shower time."

"No-"

"What?" he hesitated, eying me.

"Nothing. It's nothing." I smiled and allowed him to lead me to the bathroom.

I made a point of climbing in after him, turning my back to him as we stood under the stream. Hiding something was damn hard when you were completely naked. He had himself clean and his hair washed in minutes and the smell of seawater steamed into my senses. He turned, slipping his hands around my waist.

"Your turn," he murmured, nuzzling my neck.

I nodded and tried to slide by him, but he was much more observant than I gave him credit for. "Are you suddenly shy?"

I smiled, stretching up to wrap my arms around his neck and gave him a lingering kiss.

"No, not shy," he chuckled. "But we are, regrettably, under a time crunch."

"How regrettable?"

"You *are* very intoxicating," he said, taking my forearm and starting to pull it around his waist. Halfway there, he caught the wince. "Ariana?"

"Go on," I gave him a playful shove, "I need to get cleaned up."

But it was too late...he'd noticed the pink-tinged water in his hand and had twisted my arm out of the water stream to get a better look. The marks were once again bleeding, the jagged flesh around them swollen to a puffy pink.

"These are knife wounds. Ariana, these are knife wounds." His fingers tightened painfully on my wrist. "Where did these come from?"

"The man, at the church, he had a knife-"

"At the church? Are you fucking kidding me? Why haven't you said something?"

I dropped my eyes, uncertain of which Cole I was even dealing with...the angry one or the tender, caring one. "I was afraid for you to see."

He exhaled, long and deep. "Ariana, did you do this to yourself? The knife we found at the chapel-"

"No! Of course not."

"You've been through hell. If this is your way of coping-"

"No," I shoved him away, indignant, and stepped out of the shower to find a towel. "Fuck you, no."

He was beside me in seconds, wrapping a towel around his waist. "It's a reasonable question. A lot of people cut-"

"You are not Al. You are not reasonable."

"Wait," he managed, and this time I knew for certain his temper was flaring. "You hid this from me, me specifically...on purpose?"

"You held a gun on a priest, for chrissakes. It's not inconceivable that you would run off and start a war over this."

He looked at me as if I'd suddenly sprouted antlers. "Well, of course, I will."

"Cole-"

"If you didn't do this-"

"I didn't."

"Then it's another family trying to send a message. It's an open threat that your place as the Valentine heir is not respected. Of course, we'll go to war over that. It's not just you, Ariana. If it was done to anyone in the family, it would bring war."

"But it didn't happen to anyone. It happened to me."

"And you are a Valentine just like the rest of us and it's about time you accepted it."

He stormed off and was halfway dressed by the time I was brave enough to join him in the bedroom. He was rolling his shirt sleeves and nodded to a chair across the room.

"Sit down."

A command. I did as told and waited as he finished dressing. He finally stepped toward me, dropping to one knee and tossing a first aid kit to the floor. He grabbed my arm carefully, stretching it out over my thigh and tightened his grip - an unspoken order not to move. He cleaned and bandaged the wound then shoved everything back in the kit. "Get dressed and meet me downstairs. We're already late."

I nodded, trying not to show the crazy emotions that swelled due to his silent treatment. He headed to the door, hesitated with his hand on the knob, and then took a step back. His fingers brushed my hair, and he leaned down to kiss the top of my head. His voice was an apologetic promise that made my heart skip: "I love you, Ariana, but if you don't tell your father, I will."

CHAPTER SEVENTEEN

That took longer than expected," Cole scolded, but his hand slipped to the small of my back, welcoming me into their circle. There was no hesitation in his moves, no leftover ill feelings from my subterfuge. He understood my reasons, and he'd told me my choices...there would be no compromise.

Ignoring my father's steady glare, I twisted and pulled Cole's arm to rest under my shirt on my stomach. When I entwined my fingers with his, his body tensed against mine.

"Another one already?" he asked, low against my ear

I nodded.

He checked his watch, opened his mouth to say something but then reconsidered. His fingers began reassuring strokes on my skin as he turned back to the men. "So, what did your tests determine?"

"There are no prints."

"Not even Ariana's?" my father asked, dragging his eyes away from Cole and me.

"No, not even hers."

I had to fight the urge to say "I told you so."

"The x-rays showed nothing out of the ordinary. Expensive as hell, though. It's custom."

"If it's custom, then there is a creator somewhere that knows his own work. Find him."

"Yes, Mr. Valentine."

I let my fingers drift over the plastic bag, smoothing out the creases to get a better look. It was a beautiful craftsmanship...someone would be missing it. The scroll work was flourished with deep pits and grooves showing the detailed relief.

"Did you black light it?" A couple of the men stopped talking, and I realized I had interrupted their discussion. "Sorry," I mumbled, stepping back to Cole's side.

Franco waved off my apology. "We don't do the women are silent thing in this house. Your mother made certain of that. If you have something to say, speak up."

"I was just wondering if you tested it with a black light. Even if someone wiped it clean, the grooves are too deep on the design. Without a tool, you'd never be able to clean them out. But a black light-"

"Would pick up any traces of drugs, poisons, or bodily fluids," Cole finished.

My father smiled at me. "My daughter is brilliant. Why did no one tell me how brilliant she is? Make it happen."

The majority of the men filed out, leaving only a handful remaining. His closest associates, I assumed. I glanced around to try and memorize their faces for future reference.

"Ariana, I know we've had no time alone, and this isn't the proper setting for the very long conversation that you and I need to have."

I could sense the "but" coming on. I'd long since realized that my father had no intention of spending much time alone with me. I wasn't sure if it was because I reminded him of my mother, lagging guilt, or just because he was an asshole.

"But, I need to ask your help with something that has just fallen into my hands. Actually, that's not an accurate description. This is something that many men have died for, something that we, as a family, have worked toward for decades."

He opened his desk drawer and placed a small box on his desk. Then, one by one, he put a series of six bottles in a line. They were dark amber, their contents hidden from view, and he touched them as if they were some type of holy object.

Cole's body turned to stone around me. I knew better than to move, to draw any attention to his reaction, but my stomach plummeted with no way to try and see what he was thinking.

"These are, Ariana, the holy grail. Six vials, six families. Inside these vials are samples of each family's drug. The ones passed down; the one's men defend with their lives on a daily basis. The ones many have spent generations searching for. Ariana, these are the key to everything. Do you understand?"

I knew better than to issue the sarcastic comment that was on my tongue. Instead, I gave a slow nod and stepped forward, touching one of the bottles as if it meant something to me. It didn't. I couldn't have possibly given a damn less about his family vials, but the atmosphere in the room was so charged that I wasn't sure what else to do. "What do you want from me?"

"I...no. We, the house of Valentine, need you to tell us how to recreate these recipes. Tell us what's in each bottle and we can change the world, Ariana. I don't ask an easy task of you. These have been known to kill people. It will be a slow process, a dangerous one, and one I cannot entrust to anyone else. I believe that you alone are safe, that you have your mother's protection and blessing to save our family."

"And if not?" Cole interjected. "Would you dare risk her life for those?"

"You, even more than I," Franco hissed, "know exactly how safe she is."

Cole, Tony, and Al didn't move, but I could feel the unease washing over them. But my eyes never left my father, watching him as he shuffled around his desk before standing up and going to Cole's side. He handed the vials to one of his men and then clapped Cole on the shoulder. "I love her, too, don't forget. Come, we all need to get ready. Show off beautiful Ariana to the world tonight, right?"

He was halfway out the door with not a glance my direction.

"Wait," I stumbled forward, "wait. There's something I need to talk to you about first."

My father raised his eyes to Cole rather than me, and I had to bite back my fury. Cole motioned the other men out the door, leaving the three of us alone. I glanced to Cole, biting my lip because I really had no idea how even to start a conversation about being carved on by a madman while sitting in a pew at church.

"At the church...I mean earlier..."

But Cole was beside me again, his hand at my waist. "During the commotion at the church, someone came after Ariana."

"And I'm just hearing about this now? Cole-"

"Her safety was more important than reporting to you, Franco. Wouldn't you agree?"

"Of course, but-"

Cole extended my arm for me, putting it front of Franco to cut him off. My father was gentle, almost hesitant, and tipped the gauze away from my skin. When he got it fully removed, I could feel the fury rush through him. Cole snapped my arm back, pushing me a step behind him.

"My daughter? They dared mark, my daughter?"

"Franco-"

"Don't you try and be reasonable with me!"

"As was recently pointed out to me, when," Cole hissed, "am I ever reasonable?"

I was backing away from the two of them without even realizing it when Franco grabbed me and pulled me toward him. "Ariana, my darling, I know this has been hard. I know you are carrying more than you could have ever imagined possible. I know you feel your mother's absence with every breath and that I am more a stranger than a father to you. But I promise you, I will get them. No one will ever harm my daughter and live to tell about it. Do you understand me? I will tear their flesh-"

I tried to break free of his grasp as it continued to tighten with his threats. Cole placed a heavy hand on Franco's shoulder which finally seemed to break his tirade.

"We'll find them, Franco. Together like always, right?"

"Yes, Cole, my boy-" he trailed off, glancing at the two of us and then stumbled out the door.

One of the men hovering at the door glared at Cole. "Get that shit under control before we all end up dead."

I returned a smile he gave me, waiting until he'd left, and then turned a curious gaze to Cole. He waved to Al and Tony, motioning them to come in and shut the door.

"It's the emotions...he appears weak and distracted," Cole explained, sinking to the corner of the desk. He touched my arm lightly, frowning at the marks Franco had left behind. "It makes us look vulnerable which, of course, makes us *actually* vulnerable to attack and puts all the men on edge."

"Well, I can assure you he's not weak *or* distracted but, for whatever reason, he wants everyone to think he is."

"Your mother's death-" my scathing look stopped Cole short and caused Tony to chuckle. "Point taken. You're aware of that consideration. So, what makes you so certain it's an act?"

I tapped his leg so I could open the center drawer of the desk. I pulled out a set of vials, one by one. "Sleight of hand."

Al and Tony moved closer, folding us into a tight circle.

"Do you know how your father got his start?" Al asked, quiet, solemn. "Pickpocketing. He was a legend."

"You are well aware that I don't know that, but I do know he sent the men out with substitutes. They were in his right jacket pocket. These are the original family vials."

"We've been waiting for someone like you a hell of a long time, kid."

I frowned at him. "That's not very heartening."

Cole swept the vials off the desk and passed them to Tony. "He won't come back for them until Ariana, and I have left the office. Tony, you've got five minutes to get samples of these and get the originals back in place. Al, I need you to watch Franco and make sure he doesn't do something surprisingly ethical like change his fucking mind."

I had never seen them hesitate at an order before but they both stood still, their eyes intent on me. I pursed my lips, my eyes traveling the three of them, as I tried to figure out what was going on between them.

"Cole, you can't ask-"

"We no longer have a choice."

Al, the quiet one, the not an ounce of temper one, let out a low hiss. "Then you damn well make it 100% clear because I am not fucking her over after everything she's been through."

They both stormed out, and I scooted to sit on the desk beside Cole. "That was quite the dramatic exit. Al actually cursed."

"They have grown exceptionally fond of you," he said with a half grin.

"You are aware you invoked a five-minute time limit?"

"For them," he clarified. "You and I have all the time we need."

"Once again, not heartening."

"Come here," Cole slipped me off the desk and moved me to stand between his legs. Resting his hands on my hips, he gave me a tender kiss.

"Cole, you're scaring me."

"I need you to listen to me, okay? I'm going to ask you to do something, and before you agree or disagree, Al is right. You deserve clarity. So just breath and listen for a minute, all right? And, after, if you have questions I will do my damnedest to answer them as honestly as I can."

I moved my hand to his waist, tucking my fingers into the band of his jeans. "Okay."

"You know that your father and the house of Valentine has my allegiance. I have risked my life for him, for Teresa, and for you. That will never change. Despite that, Franco is a damned difficult man to love. He has made his own alliances and backhanded deals and has, on too many occasions, risked the lives of Valentine men for his own personal agenda. I would do nothing to harm your father purposefully, but I can't stand by and continue to watch good men, loyal men, be treated like pawns in his latest game. These families...they've operated above the law for so long that they think they answer to no one. And there are many of us who want to see that change - to make sure account-ability is brought back for everyone in equal measure." He stopped, taking a moment to rub my arms and let everything sink in. When I nodded, he continued.

"Your father didn't lie about the family vials. Many men have lost their lives to obtain them. But they didn't obtain them for him."

"They got them for you."

"No, not me. For anyone willing to try and use them to end their god complex. Frankly, no one believed it was possible...it requires too much trust. To have them all in one place, in the hands of one man-"

"A god among gods," I whispered.

"Yes, exactly. And the timing...it's so fucking suspect."

"That I don't understand."

"We didn't tell him you could identify the drugs, Ariana, but he somehow knew. He's asked you to determine the component drugs for every family recipe. Knowing those things, he could control the supply and demand, formulate stronger doses or ones that counteract, build up tolerance levels with the other side not knowing, kill off one family with another's to keep his own hands clean. If has the recipe for every family and can ac-curately recreate it, Ariana, in our world, he *is* god."

"Still not-"

"Ariana, I told you. No one has ever been able to distinguish the component drugs. In decades of manufacture, no person could accomplish what you have been taught to do, and make no mistake; you were *taught* to do it. And yet, the moment they appear all together in one house-"

"I'm conveniently available to test and provide the recipes, after being missing for over fifteen years." I staggered away from him, the weight of the implications almost too much to handle. Had my mother planned this? My father? Both of them? Did the other families somehow play a part and that's how the drugs ended up in one basket at the right time? Was it the other families that came after my mom and me and tried to prevent this? Or to get it for themselves? I tried to wipe away the tears, but it was pointless. Had anything, my whole entire life, ever been my own choice? Or was I nothing, to everyone, but a pawn to use and dispose of at their will?

"We didn't think you a commodity to be locked away, Ariana. We realized your ability was invaluable and wanted to take every precaution to keep you safe. People have killed, and will continue to kill, for these recipes."

Cole's arms engulfed me, pulling me deep into his chest and resting his head on mine. I gulped several breaths, trying to calm myself, but he stopped me. "I told you, we have as much time as you need."

It took several minutes, but I finally wiped my face with my sleeve and straightened to look at him. I wasn't surprised to see Al and Tony a pace behind him, and I shrugged away my embarrassment.

"So what are you asking? You want me to give him the wrong recipes? He's given me fake vials, so that's not really an issue."

"He would never trust his men with them," Al explained. "Have no doubt he'll approach you himself and ask you privately to help with the real recipes."

"What an awesome father-daughter bonding moment it will be," I huffed.

Tony chuckled. "That's probably the exact spin he'll put on it actually."

"So you want me to lie?"

"Nothing so simple, I'm afraid," Al said.

"This is where we really need you to be clear. Franco will be giving you a direct order, and you will be defying him. It's a betrayal of your own father, Ariana. And that is a choice that none of us has a right to make for you. It's bad enough we have to ask it in the first place."

"Betrayal assumes loyalty," I said, shaking my head. "And, unlike all of you and your precious house of Valentine blind loyalty, mine has to be earned. He has done nothing to earn it. Apparently, neither did my mother."

"That's semantics."

"No, it's not. It's the same distinction you made to me about your allegiance and loyalty if you remember. It's me believing that finding out the truth is more important than your house rules, or your street pharm business or whatever else. As selfish as it sounds, it's me wanting to find out if I have ever been more than a pawn to anybody."

"Okay, then." Al nodded which I suppose meant he believed my sincerity.

"No sampling the merchandise without me present, agreed?" Tony asked. "I've seen some of these in action and, with your system, there's no telling how it will react."

"Agreed."

"Actually, I want all of us present," Cole interrupted. "I want no question, no doubt, between any of us as to who knows what."

"The recipes…" I began but Cole shook his head.

"Are to remain in your head. Unless you have a bad reaction that requires you to tell us the ingredients, then I don't want to know. I'm not a god, and I never want to be."

"Ditto."

"I'd be a god or even like a half god. That Hercules kid got all the girls."

"When you're up to it, we'll play around in the lab and craft up some antidotes or overdose treatments…whatever you bio-chem freaks call it. It will protect the men whenever they get side-swiped."

"Or their women," I added. "Kristina or whoever else…they deserve to be safe as well and not caught up in this Valentine madness."

Al nodded his appreciation. "She'll be glad to know someone is finally worrying about her safety. Other than me, I mean."

Tony grinned. "Are you going to be our moral compass, Ariana Valentine?"

"If the family has strayed so far from protecting those they love, then somebody sure needs to be."

"Are you volunteering?"

"I think I've volunteered for enough lately."

"She's right," Cole agreed, "but if war is coming, we're going to need all the protection we can get. For everyone."

CHAPTER EIGHTEEN

I swirled my wine in the glass, toying with my mother's rosary. She had taught me the manners to get through a meal like this, but I couldn't bring myself to care about propriety any longer. The wounds on my arm fresh in their minds, Cole, and my father had refused to leave my side. Even though they barely spoke to me through dinner, they were inches from me suffocating me on both sides. I knew it wasn't intentional; they were merely on high alert for safety, but it made the whole affair nauseating.

With our "private" dinner over, most of the men were now swirling around the other families in the restaurant, making deals or accepting condolences or whatever the hell they were doing. Tony and Al were stationed beside me, both holding whiskeys that they pretended to drink.

"You two notice just about everything, right?"

"One would hope since that's our job," Al said, nodding. "Why?"

"When did my father start carrying around my mother's rosary?"

"Cole asked us the same thing." Tony frowned. "That's not a coincidence, is it?"

"I find few things are in this household," I grumbled.

"The Feast of the Assumption," Al answered. "We rarely attend mass together, but we attended the Feast as a group. He definitely had it then and every day since."

"We asked around, but no one could remember him having it before then. Doesn't mean he didn't, of course, just that no one remembers it."

"And before you ask, it's 20 days."

"What's 20 days?"

"The time between the Vigil of St. James and the Feast of Assumption. Cole wanted to know that as well."

I nodded. So, my parents had seen each other within the last month. I suppose she could've mailed it to him, but that wasn't very likely for a family heirloom. Why had she given it back? Or had he just taken it? And why didn't I know a damn thing about it?

I glanced around the room, irritated by everything. "Is it against the rule to tell me who these people are?"

"Of course not," Al smiled. "Want a crash course?"

I nodded, just to keep my mind occupied, and listened for a good twenty minutes before having to stop him. There were too many names, too many faces, too many marriages and births that intermingled the families.

"I change my mind. Cole promised me a chart. Charts work for me."

"Here." Tony sank beside me and pulled out his phone. "Will graphics help?"

He scrolled through folders of photographs until he found what he was looking for. "Six families, six symbols."

"Much easier to start with," I nodded.

"Valentine, the scroll work letter "v" and is always branded. Romano, a chained infinity tattoo although their women are marked by jewelry, not tattoos."

"Because women aren't considered permanent in their family," I guessed.

"Very good," Al said, smiling at me. "They are one of the oldest families and still pretty set in their ways."

"Skip Goretti," I grumbled. "No need to see a gunshot scar, thanks."

Tony chuckled and moved to the next photo. "Marciano tattoos a black flying eagle; the Serranos use knives to carve their initial-"

"Wait, Serrano...like Cole?"

"Yes," Al frowned. "You didn't know he was a Serrano?"

"No, I know he is Cole Serrano. I didn't know there was some rival family named Serrano."

Tony chuckled. "Guess he'll have some explaining to do before getting lucky tonight. And, last, of course, Bianchi. They use a dove, usually a white ink tattoo but also branded on occasion."

I glanced at the mark...soft, feminine, almost dainty, and so damn familiar. "Why..."

"It's why your brand is slightly different than ours," Cole said, appearing behind me and slipping a glass of whiskey into my hand. "Your 'v' has wings."

It took a few sips of the whiskey for me to put it together. "My mother was a Bianchi. Her marriage to Franco was to unite the houses. It's why the Bianchi dove was added to the Valentine rosary."

"Close," Al said with a smile of apology. "Their marriage was in *hope* of uniting the houses, but-"

"Me," I sighed. "I united the families just by being born. You, people, are so fucking medieval."

Cole chuckled and motioned Tony up so he could take his place. Even without words, he and Al were moving paces away to give us privacy.

"Don't go far," Cole ordered, "we're leaving in just a second."

"You allowed me whiskey in public which means you are steeling my nerves for something," I accused.

"Guilty. We are ready to leave, and your father is demanding to walk the Boardwalk with you. It's something the two of you did every Sunday after mass."

"This evening just keeps getting better and better."

"Ariana, he's likely to mention memories...memories you don't have."

"There's nothing new there, Cole."

"He's charismatic as hell. He can get information out of people without them even realizing it."

"Cole, I've been entrusting my life to you. Now, it's your turn to trust me. I will say nothing to endanger you or your men."

He gave me a patient smile. "I don't doubt *that*, Ariana. I'm worried about you."

"If there's one thing I do know, it's that my mom taught me how to navigate a man like Franco Valentine." I touched his leg under the table. "Besides, you promised you wouldn't doubt me again where he is concerned, remember?"

"Ariana-"

I stood up, putting my glass back in his hand. "Cole, I can't do much these days it seems but this? This I can handle."

"It's your confidence that frightens me," he admitted.

"Well," I smiled, "if my confidence is misplaced, we'll find out soon enough won't we?" I glanced to my father who was grabbing our coats and motioning me his direction. "Stay close. Promise?"

"You need never ask, Ariana."

I nodded and offered my father the best smile I could manage as I took his arm. We walked in silence for what seemed like ages, and it took me several minutes to realize he was waiting for the men to put space between us and give us privacy. When they were finally at whatever range he deemed appropriate, he finally offered me a smile. It was unnerving.

"I heard Cole had to send Marco away. You know, your mother couldn't stand his presence either. She never explained why."

It was a question veiled as an observation, but I couldn't give him an answer even if I wanted to. "You don't trust Cole's judgment?"

"Of course I do." He patted my arm. "But I trust yours, and your mother's even more."

"Was he...had he been with you long?"

"There's no need to make small talk about Savatini, child. The last thing I want is to bring more nightmares to life for you."

Interesting. So he had been told about my reaction to Marco.

"Your mother, my Teresa," he grew quieter, "can you tell me about her last moments, Ariana?"

"I'm sure you already heard the tale."

"I know of Donovan's video. I know that men came for you before Valentine men arrived. Cole, well, he was too emotional to tell me much else."

I frowned. There were so many things wrong with his words that I couldn't even process them all. That stupid video. And

Valentine men, including Cole, had arrived first. And Franco had described her death in detail while fighting with Cole. His words made no sense at all.

"Ariana," he murmured, "I'm not trying to trick you. I only hoped you'd trust me enough to share. I know Cole feels like he needs to protect you, but I've heard the men talk-"

"Oh." My thoughts finally threaded back together. "One of the men, another family...I had to...well, I shot him. He was going to kill us-"

"You need make no excuses to me. I'm sure you did what needed to be done and, at least from the gossip, you did a damn fine job of it."

"Then why-"

He sighed. "You feel guilty. It's the only reason Cole wouldn't have mentioned it...to protect you. I just want you to understand there's no need. I respect what you did. It brought you back to me."

"But not my mom."

"That was an ending never in your hands to change, Ariana."

"And my mom? How would she feel about it?"

"Your mother would do anything to protect her family. She has proven that many, many times throughout her life."

Another non-answer.

"You know, Cole, Tony, and Al are back there in the shadows."

"Yes," I nodded. "With about two dozen others."

"But it's only them that give me pause. You've grown so attached to them so quickly."

"They are good men."

"Yes. I can't deny that. Cole has always had a special spot for you, ever since you were children. Do you remember?"

"Yes." A lie of my own.

"He has grown into a man I admire and respect. He's fearless and reckless and has a temper that could split the heavens in two. I even find that a somewhat endearing trait, if I'm honest."

"But?"

"But, his history with women, Ariana-"

"Seriously? That's where you're going with this?"

"Teresa would expect me to give you guidance even if it embarrasses the hell out of both of us." He frowned. "He rampages through women and you, as my daughter, are a coveted prize to many men."

"A prize?" I hissed. "Did you just call me a fucking prize?"

"In their minds. Not mine."

"This conversation is over."

"So like your mother," he chuckled. "Getting to know you all over again is going to be a lively adventure. I'll be by tomorrow morning so we can all head to the church together."

Despite my anger, I couldn't help but feel abandoned…again. "You aren't coming home?"

"There are some people with things to answer for." He touched the bandage on my wrist with the lightest of grazes. "The men will leave you to your thoughts. When you're ready to go home, just raise your hand, and they'll be by your side."

He kissed me on the top of the head. "Be safe, Ariana. You and Cole are all that I have left."

CHAPTER NINETEEN

Everything all right?"

"Fine."

"Are you sure? You look-"

"What?"

"I don't know. Reckless."

"Defiant," Al corrected.

"It's the same one you and the old man get," Tony chuckled. "The men even have a name for it. Valentine resolution."

"No matter the outcome, the decision is made," Al agreed.

When it pertained to me, reckless and defiant were clearly not words Cole liked and he dropped his voice. "What happened with Franco?"

"Nothing important," I waved off the question. "Asked about how she died, the man I killed, waxed poetically about how your temper could destroy the heavens and warned me about how you rampage through women. That's even the actual word he used."

Tony and Al were laughing, but Cole's eyes narrowed.

"I do not-"

"I may be reckless, Cole, but his taunts don't phase me."

"Damn glad to hear it. So, what then?"

"I need a favor. You mentioned the sea glass you found in my pocket. Did you find my cell phone as well?"

"Yeah. It's in the safe back at the house."

"I need it."

"Done."

"And then I need something done quickly...and privately."

"This is starting to sound more like a Valentine mission than a favor, Ariana."

"Maybe," I relented. "I don't really know the difference, do I?"

"Okay, point taken." He tucked one hand into his pocket and leaned against the railing. "How private?"

"If I had my way, no one but you three would know."

"What kind of men?"

"Trustworthy, loyal."

"Loyal to who?"

"You. Me."

He nodded, accepting, but didn't let the insinuation against my father hang in their air for very long. "Any special skills? Theft, hacking, kidnapping, extortion-"

"Interrogation," I said, and I could see him straighten, his eyes flashing toward the two men at his side.

"I'm rarely surprised but that," he admitted, "was a totally un-expected request." He was silent a few minutes, and I assumed he was going through a list of men in his head, judging and eval-uating their abilities. "Where are Garrett and Joseph?"

"Brooklyn, I believe."

"Get them in the air. Straight to the house. We'll meet you back there in forty-five."

The men were steps away making calls on their cell phones in seconds. Cole's hand stitched to the small of my back, leading me toward the shore.

"Where are we going?"

"We are going to relax, listen to the waves, maybe make out a little under the stars, and then go take care of your business."

"Is this to be our regular thing?"

He smiled. "It calms you. Gets you out of the chaos of the house and I get time alone with you. So, yes, it will be our regular thing."

We didn't go far, still within sight of the bodyguards hovering on the Boardwalk, but far enough that the ocean drowned out the other noises. He sank, pulling me and tucking me between his knees. He wrapped his arms around my waist and dropped his head to the back of mine before letting out a long breath.

"You sound exhausted," I murmured.

"It's been a long week, yes."

"Sorry."

He chuckled. "Such a guilty conscious. I'd do it a hundred times over if it brought you back, Ariana."

"So you are a Serrano?"

"I was born one, yes."

"Are Tony and Al from other families as well?"

"Al is a lovable stray. No prior family ties. Teresa actually brought him into the family. Tony is heir to the Romano empire, although it would be war if he tried to take it."

"How did he end up with the Valentines?"

"With us, you mean?" he asked, nudging me. "It's legendary actually and not something he likes to talk about."

"If he doesn't want me to know-"

"No, it's not that. Everyone knows. It's just an ugly story. He told you the Gorettis were nuts, right? Well, he wasn't lying. We joke and say it's inbreeding, but the truth is, they've been addicted to their own merchandise for a few generations now. They're slowly killing themselves off. He was supposed to marry the youngest Goretti and tie the families together. He was sixteen, I think, and went to meet her for the first time."

"This doesn't sound good."

"He walked in and found her in bed, naked with four men. One of which was her brother. They were all so fucking stoned they didn't even notice when Tony called in the old men as witness."

"I... I don't even know how to respond to that."

"Well, depending on your proclivities, I suppose, it wasn't as bad as it looked. She didn't actually screw her brother. Instead, he'd offered her up for a gang bang and doped her up enough that she was happy to oblige. Like he said, lunatics."

"But, how did he-"

"End up with us? The three of us - Al, Tony and I - had been friends for a while by then. When the kids sobered enough to tell their story, the old men demanded that Tony still marry her and fulfill his duties as the Romano heir."

"That is so fucking fucked up," I stuttered, my hand covering my mouth.

"He came to us, nearly suicidal...he couldn't see any options left. We talked him down but still didn't have much of a solution. We just wanted to kill them all. Your father found us hidden away, got the story out of him and then, in a matter of hours, got him fake papers which added a few years to his age. He married her in a midnight ceremony and then enlisted in the Marine Corps the next day. When he left the service, he came straight to Valentine, and he's been with us ever since."

"If you tell me that there is anything like that going on in this family, then I'm-"

"Going to run far away?"

"I was thinking cut off their dicks, but sure, your idea works."

"I don't doubt you would," he said, laughing. "But no, nothing so sordid on my watch. It's why the boys make such a big joke of the-"

"Brother-sister thing between us." I shook my head. "Little shits, all of you. How does everyone know about the sex lives of other families anyway? I mean, why is that public knowledge?"

"Because every relationship can be either a threat or a solution, depending on the ties it creates. Franco, for instance, learned of our relationship from the Romanos."

"So everyone knows you are in my bed?"

"You don't realize it, but that's a very important distinction. If I had taken you into my bed, it would have been an unequivocal sign that I was moving to take over control of Valentine."

"But by being in my room-"

"You have the option to kick me out on my ass at any time. Valentine women are known to be fickle so it's expected you eventually will. I'm the problem child, remember? It's why our relationship has caused a stir, caused some anger but hasn't yet caused war."

"Over a geographic choice," I grumbled. "So ridiculous. What if I'd tried to seduce you on the beach?"

"You mean like you're doing now?" he asked, taking my hands and removing them from their traveling path. "It's not just that. It's also the way I treat you in public. Deference, respect, supportive."

"As opposed to me being servient to you. God, I am never gonna survive in this world. I'll try to be nice and bring you a drink and end up starting a fucking war."

He laughed and kissed my hand. "I won't let that happen. Promise."

"And what about you? Are you my enemy?" I asked, nuzzling his neck. "The evil rival family?"

"I am a pawn, just like you."

Taking my hand in his, he flipped my arm over and tugged at the bandage. Now that the swelling had gone down and the wounds were clean, it was easy to make out the letters carved into my skin. Or maybe it was just because I knew what to look for now.

"When you received this, I thought you understood. I should have known, of course, that you knew nothing of the family history, but I was so fucking angry that I never put that together. You are so clever that I couldn't understand why you didn't recognize it for the considerable threat that it is."

He traced the cuts, just above the skin to keep from hurting me. First the "m" and then the "s." "My birth joined the Marciano and Serrano families. As a male, I have the right to claim either family."

"Like Tony."

"Yes. It would be war, but if I succeeded, I could claim both. The "v" is more ambiguous. It could be because of my allegiance to this family, or it could be concerns of what a relationship between you and I would mean. Considering the mark was placed on you, I tend to believe the latter."

"My father as well?"

"Yes. We are, shockingly, in agreement on this."

"So, do I get to know what it would mean?"

He tightened my bandage back down and kissed me, quick and sweet. "Other than my happiness and the promise of endless orgasms?"

"So arrogant," I said with a soft laugh. "And that redirection? Not very smooth, Cole."

"You unite Bianchi and Valentine. I unite Marciano and Serrano. Together, our union would unite four of the six families. With Tony at our side-"

"It would unite all six." I sat back, considering. "Yeah, I suppose that's pretty fucking monumental. I can see why people are so edgy."

"That's all?" he laughed. "There are hundreds of men that don't sleep at night worrying about it and you act as if I just told you breakfast was going to be served a little late."

"Ah, hence the redirection. You thought I was going to have a meltdown." I touched his cheek, letting my fingers drift over his lips. "It's not my war. One day it may be. One day I may see a grand vision that would result in peace for everyone instead of constant threats. But right now? Right now, I have my own battles to fight much closer to home."

"You're absolutely right and, no matter what happens, I'm already so fucking proud of you." He kissed me hard on the lips and pulled me out of the sand. "Come on; we've got to head back. They should be there by now."

"So I don't get to know how you ended up a Valentine?"

"The quick version only," he smiled and headed us toward the house. "My parents were married to bring the Marcianos and Serranos together. With my birth, that was accomplished.

There was a huge war going on at the time between all the families. From what I understand, it was a bloodbath and my parents were in the dead center of it. It was making the news and everyone - police, Feds, locals - was starting to notice and investigate. Your father made a deal that would settle the disputes and bring peace."

"Well, that sounds smart. What was the deal?"

"He killed my parents."

I stopped mid-stride, but he pulled me along to keep us moving. "Cole-"

"Your mother was devastated. It destroyed her to have to stand beside him as he made the decision to orphan a child even if it resulted in peace and security for everyone. She threatened to walk out, but she loved your father more than life, and when he begged her to stay, she couldn't bring herself to do it. So they made a compromise."

"She got you," I whispered.

"Yes." He squeezed my waist as we stepped onto the porch. "And now that I've thrown you in an emotional whirlpool, it's time to do some business."

I nodded, straightening, and he gave me a wink of approval.

"These guys are some of the best, and I'd trust them with my life, but they are not Al and Tony. You are their boss. You don't ask. You order. No explanations. Just the facts they need and nothing more."

"Okay. Got it."

"I've got them here for you, Ariana. I don't know why-"

"I would've-"

"Told me, I know. If I'd asked, you would have. I didn't ask because, frankly, I think whatever you tell us is going to make me want to storm off and kill someone but I also know, I have no desire to leave your side."

"You're letting me take the choice out of your hands."

"As is your birthright, Ms. Valentine," he said with a mock bow. "Now, grab a whiskey and let's do this."

CHAPTER TWENTY

I stepped into the den that was my favorite and, thankfully, someone had thought to open the windows already. Tony and Al were leaning against one wall, totally relaxed, but the two new men were all business and standing at the edge of the desk.

Cole greeted them with warm hugs and then motioned to me. "Ariana Valentine, I'd like you to meet Joseph and Garrett."

I shook each of their hands in turn.

"We're glad to have you back, Ms. Valentine."

"Did I take you away from something?"

"Nothing important."

I nodded and stepped behind the desk, scooping up my phone. I clicked it on and hesitated. On the main screen, set to auto play, was the video from the bonfire. I glanced to Cole, holding the phone up his direction, and he frowned.

"I'll get that removed, Ms. Valentine," he promised. "It is down; I assure you. We just didn't consider you had a copy-"

"Don't worry about it," I said, brushing him off to continue sweeping through the photos. I finally found the series I was looking for and slid the phone across the desk to Joseph and Garrett. "I need you to find this man. Unfortunately, there's very little to go on. He was last seen on Carova Beach in North Carolina, but he will have run already. He has a few distinguishing marks which you can see in the photos."

"Can we forward these to our phones?"

I nodded and watched as they clicked several buttons before handing it back. "His real name is even in question at this point."

"We'll start with some identity databases and then go from there."

"It's going to take a while with this little to go on."

"I understand."

"And once we find him?"

"Find out who he is first and then we'll go from there," I explained. "And be careful. He's not as harmless as he looks."

They both snickered. "Always, Ms. Valentine. Anything else?"

"No one can know except-"

"These guys got it. We'll be discreet."

"Thanks."

Apparently, they took it as a dismissal because, after a quick head nod to Cole, they were already leaving. As soon as they were gone, Cole, Al, and Tony were circling me.

"28 seconds." It was a question, a statement, and an indictment all wrapped in five tiny syllables.

He thought I wanted revenge for the video...they all did. I could see it written across their faces.

"Yes but, for the record, this isn't about personal revenge."

"For the record," Tony grumbled, "we'd be okay if it were."

I smiled before turning back to the phone. "The only person I told about him was you, Cole, and I know I never mentioned his name."

I could see Cole searching his memory, but he finally nodded. "True. You didn't."

"I never told *anyone* his name."

It took a second, but I could see understanding wash over Cole, and he straightened. "Your father, on the Boardwalk, he called him by name?"

I nodded, then slid the phone to the end of the desk. "He wasn't just a 16-year-old dumbass." I tapped the screen, and the men drew closer to look.

Donovan, sitting by the bonfire in nothing but swim trunks
Flames dancing across his body in hues of red and orange
A tattoo of a black eagle, its wings spread in flight...emblazoned on
his heart

"Marciano," Tony hissed.

"When Al showed me the symbols at dinner I had a vague memory but it was replaced with the Serrano and Bianchi bombshells. After my father said his name it all clicked."

"Do you understand-"

"No, I don't, and neither do you," I said, cutting him off. "Facts not assumptions, right? So Joseph and Garrett are about to help us find out."

"Find three more men with the same skill requirements she already set. I don't want this kid slipping through. When they find him, I want to have a talk with him myself."

"Cole-"

"You aren't the only one tired of being a pawn," he growled. "Let's go to bed."

He threw my phone at Tony and Al with some nonverbal order and then led me upstairs. He was exhausted, it was written all over his body, and he was in the bed before I had even managed to get undressed. I was still fussing around the room when his grumpy plea caught my attention.

"Ariana, for chrissakes, please just come to bed."

"Sorry! I was trying to be quiet."

"You are *too* quiet. It's like someone on a stealth attack. It's fucking unnerving."

"I'll go down to the kitchen."

"No." He struggled out of bed and moved to rub my arms. "You've had an insane day, and your adrenaline is out of control. Baby girl, today was nothing compared to the emotions you'll be riding tomorrow. You have to get some sleep. *We* have to get sleep."

"Is this how you feel? Pulled in a million different directions all the time?"

"I've learned to shut things off and compartmentalize. You will, too. Come on." He tried to tug me toward the bed, but I resisted. "Ariana-"

"Cole," I murmured, "this is me throwing something at you."

He stopped and eyed me for a moment. Then he slipped his arms around my waist, linking his hands behind my back. "Tell me what you need."

"I need sleep. I'm desperate for it. I'm tired of the things spinning in my head - the lies, the betrayal, the idea that my father and Donovan are somehow responsible, how my father got the rosary…" I trailed off, shaking my head. "It's all too much. But, I'm terrified to *not* think about them, Cole, because I am saying goodbye to my mother in hours and the idea of quiet, of letting everything have a chance to flood back when every thought of her already brings me so close to hysterics-"

"Breathe, Ariana." He pulled me into his chest, rubbing my head. "Do you trust me?"

"You know I do."

"Do you trust Tony?" I faltered, and it made his entire body freeze. "What happened? Have you remembered something else? You said-"

"No, no!" I shook my head more than necessary to reassure him. "It's my mom. I told you her words echo in my head always. She told me not to trust anyone but you."

He hesitated, his voice dropping to a low rumble. "I wasn't aware of that. When did she tell you that?"

"Just before she was shot," I mumbled. "It was the last words she ever spoke to me."

"Ariana, did you come into my bed simply because your mother said to trust me?"

"No, of course not. Cole-" I lifted my eyes, but he was smiling...which made me grimace. "Okay, I get it. I can trust myself on some decisions. Yes, I trust Tony."

He chuckled then rapped on the door and waved Tony inside.

"Everyone decent?"

"Unfortunately, yes," Cole joked and shut the door. "We need some of your chemical expertise here."

Tony's eyes looked over Cole from head to toe and then turned to me and did the same. After a few seconds, they settled harder on me. "What do you need, kiddo?"

"Why does it have to be me?"

"Because cough medicine knocks him on his ass but you're a hell of a lot more complicated."

"She needs sleep, but her mind just won't slow down without making the memories go haywire. I don't want to chance a generic sleeping pill that might interact with...well, with everything else already going on in that brain of hers."

"And you want something?" he clarified. "He's not bullying you into this?"

His honest caring made my eyes rim with exhausted tears. "No, he's not. I really, really just want to sleep."

"Then no problem. Any allergies?"

"No, but I find it funny you ask *after* trying to get me to ingest 216 illegal substances."

He snickered. "Anything already in your system?"

"Two sips of whiskey downstairs and a half glass of wine at dinner."

"With the way you burn things off that is a no," he laughed. "Food or anything else *at all* on your stomach?" He gave a dark glare to Cole which caused a blush to flare on my cheeks.

"She took like ten bites at dinner and no, asshole, nothing else. Not tonight anyway."

Tony laughed as I flushed even darker. "Give me five minutes...and make sure that answer doesn't change."

Cole turned to me as soon as he was gone. "Is that really true about your mother?" he asked, soft as wind.

"Cole, Ariana. Trust only Cole. Promise me." I repeated her words, my voice breaking. Seeing the emotions running through him, it finally dawned on me that he, too, had lost his mother. In his case, it was now the third time: first his birth mother, then when Teresa ran, and now when she actually died. I reached out, flattening my palm against his chest. "After fifteen years, her last thoughts were still of you."

"Of us," he corrected, kissing me and pulling me into a comforting embrace. We were still in the same position, our own thoughts about my mom racing out of control when Tony finally returned.

He wiggled a vial in front of me. "Made special just for you. A combination of benzodiazepine and rufinamide."

"Untested? You brought her something untested?"

Tony's eyes narrowed. "I'm going to chalk that up to your cute but somewhat irrational concern over Ariana's safety and not an indictment of my talents."

I patted Cole's arm to calm him. "It's a creative solution that should be pretty damn effective. Temporarily block conscious thought, muscle relaxant, short-term sedation mixed with a drowsing agent. With an 80/20 mix, it's completely safe."

"I knew I'd have to fight him, so I erred on the side of caution and did 90/10. It'll take you a bit longer to get to sleep, but you're still talking only minutes."

"Market this to day surgery clinics and you're gonna make a fucking fortune."

"Fortunes later. Down it and get some sleep."

I swallowed the entire vial in one swig, determined to show my trust in Tony's abilities. I walked to the bed and snuggled under the covers.

"And you," Tony ordered, handing him a single pill. "Since you're such a pussy and have the tolerance level of a two-year-old, you get an OTC."

"I'm not allowing her to sleep unmonitored with a fucking anesthesia drug swimming through her system."

"And I'm not going to listen to your bitching for another 48 hours because you haven't slept. Besides, you look more of a wreck than she does, brother."

"Stalemate," I chuckled, my voice already much higher than normal. "Fortune, Tony. You'll make a fortune."

"Al and I will sit turns monitoring the two of you until the security council convenes. You're both barely gonna move. I promise."

"No."

"Ariana?"

"Hm?"

"Tell him to take the fucking pill."

"Cole, take the frolicking pill," I murmured. I heard no movement, and I sighed. "Please, Cole, take it and come to bed. I don't want to be alone anymore."

I couldn't see what transpired, but I could hear a harsh swallow and felt him dropping onto the bed beside me. His voice was a low growl at my ear. "You, Tony, are a fucking asshole."

CHAPTER TWENTY-ONE

A riana, baby girl, wake up. We need you, Ariana."
The insistent shaking grew harder, and my eyes flickered open. Cole was beside me, and the haggard look on his face made me jerk to sitting. Al was a pace behind looking, if possible, even worse.

"Al, get coffee for her. To go," he ordered, and I could hear Al shuffle away. "I'm sorry, I'm so fucking sorry, but we had no one else-"

"Stop apologizing," I grumbled. I took the clothes he handed me and started tugging them on.

As soon as I was dressed, Al had a coffee in my hand, and we were moving.

"The security council was meeting..."

"Quick facts, Father," I reminded.

"Three men at the security council had something slipped into their drinks. They all have different reactions; we can't make separate-"

"Tony-"

Cole cut me off. "Tony's one of them."

"Where are they? Take me there! Now."

The car was already waiting and running in the street. We piled inside and were moving before I remembered I had coffee. I downed half of it, the heat scalding the entire way and shaking off the last fog in my head. "How far?"

"Just a few miles."

"How long?"

"Fifteen minutes or so since the reactions were noticed," Al provided. "Ariana, one of them is really bad."

"Define bad."

"He's hemorrhaging and is really fucking violent," Cole murmured. "We have a doctor on site but, without knowing what it is-"

"The doctor can't tell?"

"He's struggling without equipment, and we can't take them..."

"Yeah, I get it. What about the other one?"

"Lethargic, disoriented, shallow breathing."

"Heart rate?"

"Slow on all except the one hemorrhaging...his is crazy high, near coding."

"You sure it was in the drinks?"

"They had nothing else, and they were clear of injection sites."

"Does this happen often?" The silence made me straighten. "Cole?"

"Not in over a decade," he mumbled.

"Is it because of me? Because I'm back?"

"There's no way to be certain." But he wouldn't look at me when he said the words.

"Lie," I hissed. "Don't ever do that again."

He nodded and took my hand in his, but still wouldn't look at me.

We were slowing to a stop, and I knew I had to prepare myself before walking in the room. "What about Tony?"

Cole flinched beside me, and I turned to Al. "Al?"

"He's unresponsive now."

"How was he before?"

"He was pretty happy, content," Cole managed. "Kept trying to play with himself and then he told someone to get you just before passing out."

"He tried to play with himself? In public? Tony?" I stumbled over the words as we got out of the car. "I will never let him live that down."

"Just let him live, Ariana. Please."

I patted Al's arm and straightened, exhaling all the stress the car ride had invoked. "I'll do whatever I can."

He nodded, accepting, and led me inside. It actually wasn't as bad as I imagined. I guess my visions had been slowly desensitizing me to violence without my even realizing it. All three were laid out on tables; chairs cast aside so the doctor could examine them. He was rushing from one to the other, barking orders. He was overwhelmed and desperate...he was apparently a friend and thought he was about to lose them all.

I went to Tony first, but he seemed the most stable. I checked his eyes, his pulse, his breathing but they all matched what I'd been told in the car. The second one looked stoned...still awake and euphoric but his body was shutting down on him even though he didn't realize it.

"He had less than the others, didn't he?"

The doctor stopped and turned my direction. "Yes. Not even half a glass. How did you know that?"

I ignored him and moved to the last man. He was completely erratic, bleeding from his nose and ears, blood trickling from somewhere on his arm. As soon as I got in his field of vision, he lunged for me, but Al had him pinned down with a single hand before he even got close.

"He's a Goretti?" I asked, turning to Cole.

"Yes. How-"

"And Tony? You said he was addicted to a bunch of substances...was heroin one of them?"

"Yes."

"I see heroin overdoses every day. This is *not* fucking heroin," the doctor spat.

"Ariana, he's just-"

"Scared to lose them, I know, Cole." I glanced over the three of them again. "It's an opiate. I'm sure of it. Do you have naloxone?"

"Yes, of course, but if you're wrong-"

"Then I just can't be wrong, can I?" I spat back. "Where are the glasses?"

"Ariana, no-"

"Cole, look at me." I touched his cheek, making sure he realized this was an argument he couldn't win. "It's Tony, and I brought this on. Where are the glasses?"

Al shoved past us, grabbed one and brought it to me. I smiled in thanks, but he didn't return it.

"You know if that kills you, he kills me, right?"

"It won't," I promised. "Tolerance of a horse, remember?"

I didn't bother to wait; afraid Cole would wrench it out of hands, and downed two giant gulps. It took a moment for my body and my brain to process it. As soon as I understood, I relaxed, knowing that they were going to be okay. Apparently, I relaxed too much because Al and Cole were at my side, both grabbing me to keep me from falling to the floor.

"You need more naloxone...a lot of it. It's acetyl fentanyl."

"I don't know-" the doctor's voice was a desperate plea for help.

"China white?" I tried. "Apache? TNT? If you tell me you guys actually call it goodfellas here, I may have a fit."

"It's an opiate," Cole clarified, finally understanding. "Fairly new street drug here in the states. Five times the strength of heroin."

I could feel it starting to burn into my system, and I closed my eyes, but Cole was shaking me.

"Naloxone, Ariana?"

"It will work," I assured him and could hear men scrambling somewhere in the room, the doctor issuing commands and instructions. "Use three or four times the normal amount for a heroin overdose. Every five minutes and keep giving it until they wake. Shouldn't take more than one or two doses for the others. They'll come out of it instantly, but Goretti-"

"He's a heroin addict," Cole guessed. "He already had tons of it coursing through his system."

I nodded and swayed. "He'll live, too. If you were wondering."

"Not on my list of concerns at the moment, no," he chuckled.

I could hear the lightness in his voice, knew he trusted me enough to know that Tony would be okay...and that was all that had really mattered.

"What about you?"

"I don't need any. I didn't consume enough. I'll burn the acetyl off in twenty minutes, tops."

"You're slurring."

I nodded, and then my eyes flashed open. Cole's arms were around me fast, holding me in place. "What is it? What's wrong?"

"Is there a separate room here?"

"An office in the back."

"Now, please, I need to be there now."

He didn't hesitate and, with a swirl of movement and colors that made me clench my eyes, he had me tucked on a sofa. I could barely feel his fingers tightening on my wrist. "Ariana-"

"Please, don't let me hurt anyone."

"What?"

"I'm so sorry...didn't think it through...so scared for Tony." I knew I was babbling, knew the tears were drenching me, but I couldn't control anything anymore...the acetyl had kicked in, and I was utterly helpless. Memories were assaulting me from a hundred different places at once...happy, sad, violent, lethal, sickening, terrorizing.

"Ariana-"

But I was past being able to vocalize anything. I could feel myself curl into a ball, could hear my own whimper as each memory flashed, but I couldn't say a single damn thing.

"Ariana!"

"Cole, move." Another voice, slow and gruff, was somewhere near.

I would hurt them, whoever it was, I just knew it. I screamed, so loudly it hurt my own ears, but still couldn't form any words.

"Get him out."

"Tony, you piece of fucking shit-"

"Now!"

I could hear the fight, the scramble and then the complete silence except for my own terrorized whimpers. I could feel myself lifted, just barely, and then felt soft brushes against my hair. They did nothing to calm me, and I bit down another scream, feeling the hot taste of metal filling my mouth.

"Scream all you want, kid," Tony's voice was soft beside me. "Goretti and Cole are making enough noise to cover up any sound a little thing like you could make. You and I? We're going to have a long talk one day. First being, did you forget opiates affect memory neurons or were you just willing to put yourself in hell to save us? Either way, you'll never do reckless shit like this again. At least not on my watch. Understand? No, I know you don't, but I'll remind you later."

I felt my body thrashing against him, but he seemed unperturbed and just tightened his grasp on me. "I know you can hear me. I know you think you're going to hurt me and want me to leave. Cole's gone. He's safe, and I can take you out with one hand so stop fighting that battle because I know there are a million others raging." As soon as I settled, his hand was back on my hair, brushing tender strokes.

"I know where you're at, Ariana. I've been there. I wondered, out on the beach that night, why you would be so willing to risk everything to get your mind to shut down. But then I realized, it was like looking in a fucking mirror. I don't know what your memories are, but I can't imagine they are much different than mine. Death, murder, rape, lies, betrayals, the loss of people you love, the hatred that consumes you over that loss...we're a lot alike, you and I. Your wars were just fought on a different battle ground.

And I know you are seeing every one of them, over and over, like a movie in your head where you can't hit the stop button. It's a living fucking hell, Ariana, but you're going to survive it and no one, not even Cole, is going to know what today cost you...unless you tell him. I promise you, kid, you are going to take on the world, and I'm going to be beside you every step of the way."

"Cole," I mumbled.

"And there she is. Look at me, Ariana."

He checked my pulse, watching and evaluating me, then smiled. "Welcome back, kid."

"That was so fucked up," I croaked and he helped me sit up. He handed me a bar towel, and I buried my face in it to soak up all the tears.

"You made the unfortunate choice of taking only a little. If you'd taken a whole glass, you would've enjoyed the ride and begged for more."

"My mistake."

"You try anything that reckless again, and I'll shoot you myself."

"But not before fondling yourself in public."

"You are a little shit," he laughed. "Let's find Cole. He's worried sick about you."

"Tony...thank you. For everything."

He pulled me toward him, touching the sides of our heads together. "I meant every damn word of it. After what you just went through, Ariana, I know there's nothing you can't handle."

Cole was on us the instant we opened the door. His clothes were torn, his face and knuckles bloody. I let him wrap his arms around me but shifted my eyes to the room.

"How are they?"

"I don't give a shit about them," he hissed. "How are you?"

"She's walking and talking, isn't she?" Tony grumbled. "Let her breathe for chrissakes."

"You and I, Tony, we are-"

"Going to table the testosterone and tell me where we are at with these guys."

"You're deflecting," Cole accused.

"Yes, I am. The rosary *for my mother* is less than an hour away so, forgive me if I'm trying to pull myself together and not be a fucking basket case. Now someone tell me something."

Al was beside us and from the blood covering him, it was clear he'd been the one to battle Cole hardest. I touched the cut beneath his eye and then ran a soft hand over the ragged splits in his knuckles.

I narrowed my eyes and turned. "Cole, did you beat up everyone? What the hell?"

"I had to get his gun away," Al explained.

"You men are so fucking childish sometimes."

"Antonio is up and moving, not even a headache. He doesn't remember much."

"Lucky him. Is he Valentine?"

"Yes," Cole answered. "And you pretty much just earned his loyalty for life, I think. He confirmed that he'd never done an opiate of any kind. That's why he was in a happy place even if it was killing him."

"See?" Tony grinned. "Happy place."

I rolled my eyes at him. "And the Goretti?"

"Carlos, I believe," Al frowned. "He's out of danger but still in pretty bad shape. I think they're going to take him home and keep dosing him there."

"Do we know who did it?"

Cole shook his head. "All the families had people here. It could have been anyone with an ax to grind against the Valentine family."

"But-"

Cole turned to me, watching me closely. He opened his mouth to ask for me to continue but Al interrupted.

"Damned disrespectful shitheads."

"Al, did you just *curse*? Is this becoming a habit?"

He nodded, embarrassed. "Today of all days to try something like this? It goes against everything."

"It is bold," Tony agreed. "But we'll worry about that later. You two," he eyed Cole and me, "need to get cleaned up and changed for the rosary. We'll clean this up here and meet you at the church."

I tensed as they walked away and Cole's hand was quick under my shirt, stroking the small of my back. He tucked himself closer to me, his voice soft. "Something you don't want to say in front of Al and Tony. What is it, Ariana?"

I turned to face him, my hand shifting to his chest. "Cole, I know your anger was out of control-"

"You want to lecture me? They beat the shit out of me to keep me from getting to you, Ariana. I think I have a right-"

"No, will you please listen?" I cut him off. "You were worried for me, angry, and I get that. It's probably why you didn't realize, but look around you, Cole. This was not an attack on us."

"Did you just say us?"

"The Valentine family."

He couldn't help the small grin that crossed his face. "Of course it was on *us*. Goretti just got caught in the crossfire."

"No." I twisted his shirt into my fist. "Really look, Cole. Valentine...Goretti...and," I nodded to Tony.

"Valentine." He shrugged but then his muscles stretched harder against the fabric of his shirt, his whole body turning to stone. "No. Romano."

"You guys, make out later! The car's waiting."

Cole nodded and straightened, leading me toward the door. "I'm leaving a security detail here."

Both Al and Tony turned his direction. "What? Why? We're-"

"I asked him to." I smiled the most innocent smile I could manage. "You know us, women. Paranoid and motherly to a fault."

"Nice save," Cole snorted as we stepped outside, "but motherly? You?"

"If anyone hurts Tony," I growled, "I *will* kill them myself."

Cole's hands cupped my face, and he pressed his lips into mine in a soft heart-warming kiss. "Welcome to *us*, Ariana."

CHAPTER TWENTY-TWO

My father was waiting at the door when we arrived, tapping his foot impatiently. "Where the hell have you two been? We're supposed to-" his eyes finally caught sight of Cole, and it was impossible to miss the concern wash over him. He stepped to him, his hands flying to Cole's head and traveling down his body to check every wound. I couldn't help but be jealous - my father hadn't even bothered to see me for days. "Cole, what happened?"

"Ariana, can you-"

"Yes. Go get a shower. I'll be up to change in a minute." When he hesitated, second thoughts about leaving us alone, I scowled and waved him away and turned to my father. "Somewhere private?"

He nodded and, taking my arm, led me to the back office. I moved to the windows that I loved, the ones already thrown open and letting the sea breeze flow.

"That was your favorite place when you were little. Do you remember?"

There was something in his voice that told me he already knew I didn't. "No, I don't. I don't remember much actually. I was so very young."

He kissed the back of my head as he moved to sit on the window seat. "Thank you for finally telling me."

"I can tell you it's my favorite place now, though."

"Was he fighting for you?"

"You love him, don't you?"

"Yes," he clipped without hesitation. "He's been a son to me for a very, very long time. To me and your mother."

"Then why," I asked, sitting down beside him, "is it so inconceivable that I would love him as well?"

"When you were tiny, your mother saw it. She warned me then, you know, but I was too stubborn to listen." He brushed a tendril of hair from my face. "You'd die for each other, Ariana, and then I'll lose you both."

"Stop worrying about that and enjoy having us here. Isn't that a Valentine rule? Living in the moment or whatever?"

"No," he chuckled, "that's a Serrano rule."

"Well, it's all starting to blend, isn't it?"

"Yes, it certainly is."

And he clearly wasn't happy about that idea. I cleared my throat. "Speaking of, there was an attack at the security council."

"What?"

I explained the morning's events and, even though I wasn't sure Cole would approve, I told him of my theory that the attack was actually against Tony.

"He is heir to two families, but he's been that for a very long time. Why now? It's a good theory but doesn't make much sense."

I stretched my bandaged arm to lay across his lap. "Does this make any sense?"

"No, it doesn't," he agreed. "Unless-" His eyes narrowed and darkened and I could almost see his emotional switch turn off and go all business. It was frightening to watch, and I stood up to scoot away from him.

"Unless what?"

"Someone is trying to realign the families, to shuffle the power where it benefits them most."

"War."

"Not yet," he corrected. "A person would be stupid to start a war without all the pieces perfectly aligned first. But, yes, it does look like someone is trying to prepare for it."

"Who?"

"Until we know more, your guess is as good as mine, darling."

And that, that one little term of endearment said in his most businesslike voice is how I knew he was lying. I smiled and motioned upstairs. "I've got to change."

"Yes, we're running late, and Father Michael will not be pleased."

I was almost at the door when I turned and leveled a gaze at him. "You'll protect Tony?"

He looked offended that I even asked. "Of course. I'll protect all of us, Ariana. That's what I do."

That, I did believe. He *would* protect us...no matter what that might take, and that scared the hell out of me.

When I made it upstairs, Cole was almost finished getting dressed. He rarely wore suits and, for the briefest second, the sight of him took my breath away...and not in a good way. I whirled, turning away from him and moving to the chair where he'd laid out my dress. I gripped it tight, willing my breath to return to normal.

"Did something happen with Franco?" he asked, already behind me. "What's wrong?"

I shook my head and began tugging off my clothes to get the dress on. I stumbled several times, and he put a hand on my back to help me. "Ariana, if he-"

"It's you. It's the suit." I tried to wave him off as I stepped into the dress. "You look like them...the ones that always came for us."

"I'll change."

"No, don't be ridiculous. I'll be surrounded by hundreds of them today. I better get used to it now."

"You seem..." he sought for the word, "overly sensitive, emotional. Is it the acetyl?"

He was right. I still had memories whirling, the excitement from the overdoses, the veiled conversation with my father and the talk of war...everything seemed to be colliding all at once. I tried to stop the tremble in my hands. "PMS," I joked but then saw how truly worried he was. "Maybe ask Tony? I'm not certain, but you're right. Everything is all off kilter."

"I'll call him from the car. Your father?"

"Loves you like a son. Ask me about the rest later, okay?"

He nodded and reached to hand me my shoes just as a knock sounded on the door. "Come in."

My father was there, and I assumed he came to hurry us along, but he stood still, his eyes on Cole. "I've added more security to Tony. I'm doing the same for Ariana and yourself."

"Me?" Cole frowned, and I could see the argument ready to fly.

"Why?"

Franco looked my way as if just noticing my presence. "The first attack was on you, heir to two houses. The second was on Tony, heir to two houses."

"They're marking all the heirs," I murmured, my eyes darting to Cole.

"So I'm next." He looked completely nonplussed. He even shrugged. "Let's get to the church. You can put your shoes on in the car."

"Cole-" My father reached for his arm.

"Threats don't scare me, Franco. You've raised me with a hell of a lot more *loyalty* than that."

It was a message, but I couldn't figure out if it was for me, my father, or perhaps even both. We were halfway down the stairs, and I was still puzzling it when I stopped and realized my brain was really not functioning right. "I forgot her rosary."

"We're late, Ariana-"

"It's *her mother's* wake, Franco," Cole scolded. "I don't think they'll start without her."

"I'll meet you in the car."

I was searching through the dresser when Cole appeared behind me, his hand heavy at my waist. "What's the matter?"

"I just forgot it. I can't go without it-"

"Ariana," Cole grabbed my hands, tightening them into fists. He pulled up the sleeve of my dress where the rosary was tightly wrapped around my wrist. "You put it on earlier so you wouldn't forget it."

"We can go, then. It's okay." I nodded and began tugging him back down to the car.

"The talk of heirs being at risk- did that scare you?"

"No, yes. I mean, I don't want you hurt obviously."

"No one is at risk, Ariana. You, Tony, and I are all perfectly safe."

"How do you-"

"There's only one family with enough power to challenge all the others. Only one with enough confidence to mark the heirs as a message *to the other families* of their intention to take control."

I stopped at the door to the car, my hand landing on the hood as I tried to steady myself from the emotions flying through me. "Ours," I whispered.

"Yes, baby girl. Ours."

CHAPTER TWENTY-THREE

Hey, kid." Tony sank down at my knees as soon as I had been led to the front pew. "Cole asked me to take a look at you. Want to tell me what's going on?"

"It's like everything in my brain is firing at the same time."

"You seem to be containing it pretty well."

"I think he's worried I won't."

"Well, fuck him. You're allowed to act however you want today."

I smiled and continued to finger the rosary in my lap. Tony's eyes traveled down to watch me.

"You know you're trembling, right?"

I nodded.

"But you can't make it stop?"

I shook my head.

"Did you tell him about earlier? About the memories?"

"We didn't have time. Franco hasn't left our side."

"You mean your father."

"Yes. What did I say?"

He smiled. "Doesn't matter. Were you going to?"

I opened my mouth and closed it again. The truth was, I had no idea how even to try and explain the hell that drug had put me through much less try to organize the memories in some manner than made sense. Was it fair to Cole? No. Was it all I could do to try and hang onto sanity? Yes.

"Hey," Tony tapped my knee. "Your guilt complex is wicked sensitive, isn't it? Stop judging yourself. Listen, I'm going to be right across over there. If you need to get out of here at any point, you just lift up that rosary, and I'll have you out. Okay?"

I nodded just as Cole settled in beside me. He took my hand in his. "What's the word?"

"Just stress, I think. She's disassociating to try and make it through the day." He knew I was about to object, so he cut me off. "Which is totally okay and completely understandable."

"And the prescription is?"

"Sleep and actually giving her breathing space to mourn her mother's death. In the meantime, just keep her mind on something other than the lengthy speeches they are going to give about Teresa up there. We all already know how amazing she was so there's no need to hear the poetics."

"Will do, boss." Cole gave him a mock salute as he walked away and then he snuggled closer to me.

"Cole, I'm scared."

"You are fearless."

"Not right now I'm not."

"What is it then?"

A million things, I wanted to say. But the truth was, at this exact moment, there were only two things important enough to mention: "Being alone and the quiet."

He sighed. "Tony, Al, Antonio, Garrett, Joseph, Franco - you have an ever-growing list of people who would die for you, Ariana, and I love you more with every breath. You are anything but alone."

"And the quiet?"

"I've been thinking about that for a while actually," he smiled. "And I have a plan." He tugged my arm into his lap and pulled up the sleeve of my dress just enough to show my wrist.

He traced a capital letter "A" in slow, deliberate strokes. "Acetyl fentanyl."

He traced the letter "B." "Butalbital."

He traced the letter "C" just as my father dropped onto my other side. I tensed, but Cole merely smiled and patiently redrew the letter.

I squeezed his hand. "Cocaine."

It took six trips through the alphabet before the closing prayer finally signaled our release. I hadn't heard any of the eulogies or speeches about my mother, and I knew she was fine with that. She'd run from all of these people - she wouldn't have given a damn what they had to say now.

I had struggled to be social, accepting condolences and best wishes or whatever they mumbled to me, but I just couldn't do it. In the gathering hall, hundreds of people from warring families were acting as if peace was the most important thing in the world. Even I was smart enough to know they were plotting behind each other's backs but, that seemed to be ignored for the "sake of Teresa." It was more than I could stomach and, as they started in on plates of finger foods, I dropped back into the shadows to find my retreat. Knowing Father Michael was making deals of his own in the hall, as soon as I spied his office, I clambered inside to try and catch my breath. I'd only managed a few minutes before the soft click of the lock made me whirl.

"He hasn't taught you not to slip away yet, has he? But I hear he's teaching you lots of other things."

"Marco-" I hissed, backing away. Was it okay to scream in a church? Would anybody even hear me over their ridiculous party for my mother's death? "Cole-"

"Yes, precious Cole," he smiled as he moved toward me. "Do you think he'd shoot me in a church?"

"Yes, yes I do."

"Fucking mercenary that kid."

"What do you want?"

"Now that hurts." He closed in on me in two strides, backing me toward the wall. "It's true, then? That you really remember nothing?"

"I-"

"You won't scream," he threatened. "We know each other much too good for that, don't we? You'll remember, littlest Valentine. I'll make sure of that."

And I did. As soon as his hands were on me, his mouth brutally assaulting my throat, everything came flooding back. Visions of he and my mother...over and over. Visions of him coming for me...no matter how hard she fought. The touches from the past blended with the present and I wretched all over him. He didn't care. He didn't even hesitate as he tried to claw at my dress, his hands puncturing into my thighs. I whimpered but, he was right, I was too terrified even to scream. I began grabbing things within reach, hurling them at him.

"You've learned to fight," he growled, "that will make this even more fun. Just like Teresa."

"God's mercy-"

Father Michael's hand was on his mouth, but I didn't wait for any other opening.

I lunged into the gathering room, gasping for air, desperate for a way outside. Across the room, Cole and my father were in deep conversation. I willed them not to see me but, as if called, they both looked my direction at the same time. My body convulsed, black spots flashing across my vision. They were both headed for me, but I did a fast pivot, shoving through the crowd and out the side door.

As soon as I hit fresh air, I was running toward the house, flinging the door open. Alarms sounded, men came running with guns drawn but then backed away when they recognized me. I flew up the stairs to the closest bedroom, sliding across the floor on my knees and retching into the toilet. Dozens of footsteps pounded on the stairs, and I could feel them all hovering at the door. They parted, allowing Cole and my father to enter. They took a step toward me, and I shoved myself into the wall, sending a tray of something clattering down over my head.

"Ariana," my father's voice was soft and warm. A tender, calming tone that I could believe he'd used with me as a child. He tried to step toward me but I jerked again, and he put his hands up in surrender. His voice, although still tinged with concern, was a clear order: "Tell me, Ariana."

I could barely speak, could barely manage to say the words out loud through my broken sobs. "He raped her. Over and over. For years." I pulled my knees to my chest, rocking myself. "Daddy, he raped her."

"Who?" he demanded.

"Marco. It was Marco."

My father turned, barking orders as he stepped out of the room. "Now. I want him here now! Take everyone and drag that sonofabitch out of the church."

While my father raged, Cole had moved toward me. Kneeling in front of me, he reached out slow, touching each individual mark on my arm. He tilted my head, tracing the shape of Marco's fingers on my throat. "And what about you?"

"No. You know he didn't."

"There are a hundred ways to rape someone," he hissed. "Ariana, look at me."

But I couldn't. Scuffling and screaming, angry, hate filled words assaulted my ears from the hall: they'd found Marco.

"Ariana!" Cole shook me, demanding my attention.

"Cole," I whispered, "I was just a tiny little girl...the littlest Valentine."

And he was gone. I lunged at him but missed. I scrambled to my feet making chase. I tried to break through the crowd, but Tony grabbed me around the waist, holding firm...the only time I could ever remember him touching me without permission. Marco stood in the center, spouting vile things about my mother and me but it only lasted seconds: with no patience for words, no forgiveness for begged excuses, Cole, and my father raised their guns and fired in silent unison. Two bullets in his head, blood splattering everywhere and then Marco dropped to the floor.

I tried to wriggle free, but Tony held tight until Cole gave him a nod, granting me freedom. His release was so instant that I stumbled to the floor. I picked myself up and rushed to Cole, wrapping my arms around his waist and burying my head into his chest. He wrapped one arm around me while tucking his gun away with the other. "Clean this up," he ordered and swept me out of the room.

CHAPTER TWENTY-FOUR

As soon as we were alone, I was stripping everything off and heading toward the shower. Thankfully, a knock at the door stopped his pursuit, and I locked myself in the bathroom before Cole could follow. I could hear my father's voice, worried and low, and knew I didn't want to know whatever they were saying. I turned on the shower as hot as I could stand and climbed inside, letting the water assault my skin. I scrubbed, trying to get the scent of Marco off me, to remove the touches and memories all at the same time. I was still scrubbing when Cole pulled the curtain open and turned off the water.

"I locked the door," I mumbled.

"Did you expect that to stop me?" he growled. "Get out."

"No, I-"

"You've rubbed your skin raw, get out."

"Please stop yelling at me," I begged.

He froze, and I could see the confusion on his face. He was so consumed with his anger at Marco that he didn't even realize he was lashing out at me.

"Cole, please."

He took a shuddering breath and reached behind to get me a robe. He extended his hand, helping me out of the shower and wrapping the robe around me. I headed to the bed but stopped, seeing a bottle and syringe on the nightstand. My fingers traced the ornate V on the white label.

"Franco. He didn't know what to do. He thought it would help you forget."

I nodded. "He doubts everyone, but he believed me without question."

"Of course he did," Cole admonished. "He's your father."

I climbed into the bed, leaning against the headboard and tucking my knees to my chest. My regular defensive position it seemed.

"You want a drink?"

"Are you going to lecture me?"

"Not tonight."

"Then, yes. Several."

He moved to the door and mumbled a few words. There were apparently still a dozen men on the landing. He had the whiskey in hand quickly and was back at my side, pouring me a glass.

"None for you?"

"Fueling my emotions with alcohol right now would have devastating results."

I took a drink, but my stomach lurched. I took a few breaths and tried again but this time, as soon as the smell drifted to my face, I gagged hard enough to shake my whole body. I sat it on the table and shuffled down in the bed, curling onto my side and hugging a pillow as the tears started to fall. Cole knelt beside the bed, his hands scalding hot against my cold ones. "Tell me what you need."

"Just don't leave."

He stripped off his jacket and shoes then shuffled over me, curling up behind me and tugging me into his arms.

"I have no one."

"Ariana, you've always had me," he whispered.

His words were sweet and meant to calm but, in the quiet, the visions of everything began to flood back. I tried to fight back the hysteria I felt building, and I began rubbing my arms through the robe.

"Baby girl," he murmured, "what are you doing?"

"I can still smell him on me. Everywhere."

I knew it was irrational but, thankfully, he didn't point that out. "You want to try the whiskey again? A bath, maybe?"

I shook my head and jerked away from him. I was on the floor, pacing before he'd even managed to sit up. I felt jittery, each memory sending fire through my veins as if it had just happened. I stood in the middle of the room, swaying without meaning to, and could hear my own teeth chattering.

"Ariana-"

I lurched away from his touch, my body ramming into the edge of the table. I was halfway to the floor before I managed to catch myself. He was closing in on me, and I shuffled away every muscle trembling. He wanted to hold me still, calm me, but the thought of not moving was suffocating. I tried to pour a glass of water, but it shattered to the floor, broken pieces of glass circling my bare feet.

"You are scaring the shit out of me here," he argued, reaching for me again.

I batted his hands away. "I'm fine. Really. I just keep seeing things, memories. They are blinding, they won't stop."

"Other than Marco?"

"Yes. No. I don't know. It's a jumbled mix." I began rubbing and scratching my arms again, my feet crushing into the glass. I could see the blood start to flow, but I felt nothing and, curious,

I began to make purposeful steps on the shards just to see what would happen.

"Stop moving!"

"I can't," I whimpered, my chattering teeth and the crunch of glass echoing in the room. I glanced at him, seeing the absolute fear on his face. It was so much like my mother - the exact same look she'd give me each moment before we'd run. I let out a broken sob and dropped to my knees, burying them in the glass. "Cole, please, I don't understand what's happening."

"Did he give you something? You'd know, Ariana. Think, did he make you take something?"

"I don't want to think."

"You have to. Concentrate, Ariana. Please."

I rocked as I allowed the memories of Marco to cross my mind. His touch, his mouth, his hands between my thighs, his threats, and fury. They were sickening but, as if I was watching it happen to someone else in a movie, I felt nothing. I shook my head. "No."

"No, he didn't?"

"No, he didn't." I nodded, somehow managing to get to my feet, and began yanking off the robe. "Why is it so fucking hot in here?"

He shoved the robe back on me before I could surge away. "For chrissakes, you're freezing." He stepped away, two hard raps against the door. "Tony. I need Tony."

I smiled. I liked Tony. He was nice. But then I realized he'd see me like this and I started shaking my head. Combined with my jittering, I knew I probably looked like I was convulsing but I couldn't bring myself to care.

"Too hot," I grumbled. I tried to pull the robe off again, but Cole was next to me, stopping me. I began to thrash at him, and he picked me up, locking me into his arms and lowering me to the ground.

Visions assaulted me of this exact same position - me or my mother I had no idea- and I began punching and kicking him. Cole straddled my hips, pinning me down and locking my arms to my chest.

"What the fuck?" Tony's voice was hard as he slammed the door behind him.

I glanced around to try and see what he saw: shards of glass, blood on me, on Cole, me pinned to the ground under the full weight of his body. "He didn't do it, I swear. He didn't hurt me. Promise."

"He loves you. I would never have believed that he did." He moved to kneel at my head, his eyes boring into mine. "World stop spinning for you, kiddo?"

"She's in some terrorizing loop. I thought it was an overdose, but she swears he didn't give her anything."

Now that I knew Tony wasn't going to kill him, I sank back into my own world. "Please, please let me up," I begged. "It makes it so much worse."

"Ariana, I'm gonna touch your throat for just a few minutes, okay?" Tony asked. When I didn't answer, he snapped his fingers to get my attention. "Okay?"

I clenched my teeth to stop the tremors long enough to respond. "Yes, okay, okay."

His fingers were on my throat, tapping out a count. "Cole, she's like ice."

"I know," he growled.

"All done, kiddo," Tony promised taking his hand away. "Her heart rate is through the fucking roof."

"I didn't bother to check. I can hear it." He loosened his grip just enough to let me start rubbing my arms again.

"How long has she been doing that?"

"Since the shower. She kept saying she couldn't get him off her."

"You're sure he didn't slip-"

"Yes."

"Please," I begged, twisting to try and get loose. "Just let me move, please."

Tony brushed my forehead in slow, even strokes. "We're gonna help you, I promise. Just bear with us. We don't have the legendary drug-sniffing skills you do. Let her up."

"What-"

"Cole, if you want to help her then stop the blind hatred at Marco and let her up."

I was loose in seconds, up and pacing, jittering, chattering, trembling everywhere.

"Look at her, brother," Tony said his voice a low command. "She's not od'ing; she's withdrawing."

"No, she's had nothing-"

"Look at her!"

I could feel their intense gaze on me and offered them a half smile. I nodded as if they'd asked a question.

"It must've been happening for days. She was probably nearing the edge last night when we gave her the sedative, and then the acetyl interfered today. We've both just been too fucking blind to see it. It would explain why the visions are coming faster and stronger, the mood swings, the lack of appetite, the-"

"I don't care. Just tell me what it is."

"Something psychoactive, obviously, but I don't know."

Cole's voice was a broken plea. "Tony, it's gonna kill her."

"We could try methadone."

"No." I shook my head. "Effective on opioids only."

"In fucking withdrawal and she's still smarter than the two of us put together."

"You're right," Cole murmured, "she is." He was beside me fast, looming over me but not touching me.

"Ariana, look at me." He commanded. I obeyed. "I need you to name a drug for me, can you do that?"

"Coffee?"

Tony was on my other side. "All you want, kid."

"Okay, then."

"Either liquid or powder. Low dosage. Able to be spiked without notice."

"Buildable tolerance," Tony added. "Psychoactive. Fucks with your head."

"Valentine," I smiled as I continued to rock on my heels. "That's an easy one."

"She's right," Tony grimaced, "we just described our own fucking drug."

"No. Close but no." Cole shook his head. "It doesn't only fuck with your mind. It screws with your memories specifically. Valentine makes you forget. This makes you forget some things while making others less intense emotionally but more vivid physically. Not deja vu but more like..." he trailed off, his eyes closing. He shook his head and exhaled. Then I heard the words I'd said to him over and over: "like a movie playing in your mind."

"Valentine plus propranolol."

"And it's sweet, isn't it?"

"Yep."

"Fuck, fuck, fuck." Cole was moving around the room, gathering his shoes, keys, jacket.

"What is that?"

"It's a PTSD drug. The one they give returning combat vets."

"PTSD again," he mumbled. "Do we even stock that?"

"No, but I know where to get some."

"Sweet?"

"Fucking Teresa," he growled. "She's been dosing Ariana's coffee with it since she was a kid."

"Cole's coffee is much better than mom's. Hers is always sweet straight out of the pot."

"Watch her. Do not leave this room. Ten minutes tops."

"We'll have ourselves a party, won't we, kid?"

I nodded. "Tony's fun. I like Tony."

CHAPTER TWENTY-FIVE

I awoke feeling normal. A real normal like I hadn't felt since before my mother died. I lay still, foggy memories flittering in and out as I tried to figure out what was real and what was imaginary. I rolled over, watching Cole, Tony, and my father as they sat huddled in the corner of my room talking in hushed voices. Even they seemed normal. Like a family. Cole's eyes met mine, and I offered him a smile. He nodded my direction and my father was beside me in two long steps.

"Ariana," his kiss was feather light on my forehead. "I was afraid I was losing you, just like-"

"You lost my mom," I murmured, patting his hand. "It's okay. I still remember way more than I'd like to."

He brushed my hair out of my face. "You look so very much like her."

"Unfortunately, that is exactly what Marco thought."

"He is-"

"Dead. Yeah," I cut him off. "I remember that as well."

"I've missed your whole life, Ariana. I'm so very sorry for that."

He looked so broken, so very close to tears, and I could see why my mother fell in love with him. But, unlike her, I wouldn't be blindsided. I knew what he was capable of, and I refused to let myself forget that. I patted his hand. "Then we'll just have to meet each other all over again. Dinner, a real family dinner, tonight? Cole, Al, Tony?"

"Anything you want, it's yours, darling." He leaned down and kissed my forehead again. "You are so strong, so beautiful, so much more amazing than I ever realized you could be. You and I, Ariana, are going to change the world. Welcome home, my sweetest Ariana."

He stepped away and Tony took his place. "We're going to have that long talk sooner rather than later. But we'll make it a tequila date. There's this nasty rumor going around that you have a tolerance level that beats even mine."

"Destroying your reputation with the boys?"

"Fuck yeah," he laughed and ruffled my hair. "Go easy on my brother there." He nodded toward Cole. "You scared the hell out of him."

"Duly noted." As Tony left, my eyes drifted to Cole, but it was impossible to determine his mood.

"Come here."

"You come here."

"Is that an order, Ms. Valentine?"

I smiled. "Meet you halfway?"

He was there, waiting, before I'd even struggled out of the bed. I got my balance and then made my way to him. I wrapped my arms around his waist, snaking my body against his. His hand was in my hair, his face at my throat as he inhaled me. "There are so many things we need to discuss. Your father, your mother, Marco, Valentine pharmaceuticals, those memories you still don't want to tell me-"

"Not now." My hands slipped under his shirt, my nails scratching a path up his chest. "I didn't know if I was going to ever get to touch you again, Cole, so today, you owe me a lesson."

I ignored his penetrating gaze, tugging his shirt up enough to get my lips on his skin. He still didn't react so I buried my nails into his back, jerking him toward me. That *did* get a reaction, and he tugged his shirt off and tossed it aside. My teeth buried into his chest, but before I could try again, his hand was tangled in my hair and pulling my neck back to assault my mouth. He paused long enough to yank my shirt over my head and then his mouth was on me, a trail of intense fire down my neck. He jerked me forward, taking my breast deep in his mouth. My nipples puckered, hard and thick under his tongue as he flicked them. His hand cupped the other, squeezing and pinching until I yelped from the pain and pleasure of it. His fingers continued down, slipping under the edge of my underwear and going straight for my opening. He didn't hesitate and thrust his fingers inside, fast and deep. My knees buckled, and he tightened his arm around my waist to keep me from falling. He gave a low chuckle as he continued to push inside me. "Always so fucking wet, Ariana."

"For you, Cole. Only for you."

"First lesson?" he growled as he began to undo his pants, "that was the perfect thing to say."

Before he could step out of his pants, I had his cock in my hand. I stroked him, long and slow, as he backed me toward the bed. He pushed me down, and his lips were on my throat. "Remember, don't scream."

"It's my house. If I want to scream-"

"In *your* house, your screams will bring a dozen armed men to our bedside," he grumbled. "Don't scream."

He didn't wait for a response, knowing I would obey. His mouth lit a fiery trail down my skin as he moved down to my thighs. He breathed hot on my sex, sending chills through me, before taking it in his mouth. His tongue traced my folds, pushing inside me and tracing circles around my opening. I grabbed the sheets as he suckled my clit, then flicked it and I realized he was gauging my reaction to his every move. He continued to circle my clit with his tongue until it swelled and then he scraped his rough stubble across it. My body lurched toward him, ripping sheets as I moved. "So," he chuckled, "rough it is."

"Cole, please," I groaned in frustration.

He ignored my plea, his tongue thrusting back into me and I spread my legs wider to give him better access. I could hear him lapping my juices, his own soft moans starting to mingle with my own. His tongue traced down to my ass, circling there, plunging gently and my body rocketed off the bed, wanting more. "Mm," he groaned, "time enough for that lesson a later day, baby girl."

"Cole!"

He raked against my clit again, harder and faster this time. My hand went to his hair, trying to force him even harder into me but he broke my grasp and moved to straddle me. My hands circled his cock without instruction, spreading his own slickness down the shaft. He grabbed my arms, locking them above my head just as he shifted to get his body between my legs. "Tell me what you want."

"You. Inside me. Now."

His hands gripped my hips, arching them off the bed. He slid his tip inside and then out again, resting it on my clit. I wiggled for more, but he held firm. He did the same again, teasing me.

"All of you, Cole."

He thrust deep without warning, and I yelped. He gave a slow, gentler push but I buried myself down on him, needing him far inside me. He dropped to rest on his forearms, touching my face to get me to look at him. "I won't hurt you again, not without permission. Tell me how you want me, Ariana, and I'm yours."

"Fuck me, Cole. Hard. Harder than you've ever fucked anyone else."

He thrust into me, our bodies sliding from the power behind it. And again. But it still wasn't enough. "Deeper, please, deeper."

He snickered. "I go any deeper, and I'm going to end up in your throat, Ariana." He shifted, grabbing my legs and wrapping them around his middle. Then he grabbed the headboard and plunged into me. A whimper escaped, and my hands went to his back, nails burying into his flesh. He continued to pound me, our bodies slapping together as he drew farther and farther inside me. I could feel myself coming and locked my legs around him, arching my pelvis to get more of him. This time, even he felt the difference.

"Christ," he groaned, delving into me the same way again. His voice was broken, gasps of unexpected ecstasy. "Damn...baby girl...so fucking tight...fuck." He was faster, thicker, and knowing he was coming sent me over the edge. I felt the spasms wrench him further into me, pain and ecstasy blending together. When he came, seconds later, I could feel his throbbing reaching longer, seeping into my very being. He patted my legs, signaling me to let loose, and then he dropped onto the bed. It was several minutes before either of us could move, and he rolled to give me an exhausted kiss before pulling me to rest on his chest.

"So, my little virgin likes it rough."

"You weren't complaining a minute ago," I said, biting him playfully.

"God, no. That last move you made, you rubbed my cock raw, Ariana."

"You have a filthy mouth."

He laughed. "You weren't complaining a minute ago." His fingers drifted over my nipple, toying with each one. "I can't wait to take you somewhere you can scream."

"Can we do that? Go somewhere? Away from all this?"

"You want to run?" he asked, disbelieving.

"No, just...the chaos of this place. It's all too much, too soon."

"Is that directed at me, us?"

"I want to go away *with you*, Cole, so that should alleviate your insecurity. You really are not very observant, are you?"

"You're observant enough for both of us," he assured me. "A long weekend away? A romantic escape, is that what's in your head?"

"I'm not much of a romance girl."

"I don't know. 'Fuck me deeper' was a pretty sweet phrase to hear."

"You are incorrigible."

He pinched my ass as he laughed then snaked his arm to rest against my hip. "And where would we go?"

"I've been thinking about that."

"I'm not surprised."

"How about New Orleans?"

He hesitated, and I could feel his body twitch in my arms. "Why there?"

"Why not?"

"Ariana."

I rolled onto him, folding my arms across his chest and resting my head to look at him. "It was the only place my mother and I lived more than once. You keep talking about how brilliant but devious she was."

"Devious is your word."

"Whatever. It's true. I keep thinking that she would have keep notes, a journal or something. It's the most basic rule of science. Recipes that worked, ones that failed, and maybe-"

"What she was trying to accomplish with you. I've considered that myself. She was meticulous. We found her records after she fled, so it makes sense she started recorded things again."

"They could've gone up in smoke when you burned the house down but, if she is as smart as you say, there would've been copies. She wouldn't have wanted to be caught with them."

"It makes sense," he acknowledged, but I could still feel the tension etching through his muscles.

"We know she still had Valentine men in her life and, somehow she managed to come up with the money to keep dosing me."

"We talked about that the first time you mentioned it. It made us wonder if she wasn't pulling Valentine funds from somewhere. Or Bianchi even. Al's been checking but so far found nothing."

"If it's there, I'm sure he'll find it," I nodded. "So, why *not* New Orleans?"

"It's not Valentine territory. It's a no man's land of people trying to take control of the port, the city. A couple of years ago, some of the guys went down for Mardi Gras. No business just letting loose. Only two made it back. It's violent on any given day but visiting? It's a signal that we intend to take over."

"But if it was just the two of us-"

"I would never go there without an army at my side. Two if you're beside me."

"So it would be war," I sighed in defeat. "I get it. I'll try and think of somewhere else she might have left them."

"You said it yourself," he murmured, twisting the ends of my hair in his fingers, "it's the only place she took you more than once."

"Then I'll let your pharmacy guys start lab ratting me again. It's fine, Cole."

"No," he sighed, "it's not fine. Your mother didn't erase your memories. In fact, she took considerable care *not* to erase them and only hide them. And that means-"

"She would've created a way for me to retrieve them. If I ever wanted them."

"Or needed them," he corrected. "Her life revolved around the house of Valentine, both the good and bad of it. It's much more likely that she thought you would need them at some point. Either for your own protection or the protection of the family."

"It makes me wonder what else is in my brain. It's not like she just hid some traumatic event when I was a child and still living in the household."

"Like Marco," he growled.

"Yes," I rubbed his chest to get him to calm again. "That one is understandable if not a little self-serving on her part. It would be hard to go unnoticed on the run with a little kid constantly having meltdowns."

"And that's why she turned to the PTSD drugs. They were already known to be effective. Adding them to Valentine to get the exact result she needed was brilliant."

"But there are other memories of much more recent events that she hid as well. The man in California, my birthday party."

"The training she gave you on the drugs."

I nodded. I hadn't thought of that one. "I wonder why I can't remember her training me, but I can still recall everything I learned."

"Tony and I talked about that. He thinks it's because your recognition is based on a physical response, not a mental one. You need to actually see, smell or taste the drug to identify it. If Teresa's drug worked differently, taking out your physical memories, you could have easily forgotten how to breathe."

I settled down heavier in his arms, a rush of thoughts making me close my eyes. My mother was brilliant, but the risks she took were just unfathomable to me. How many people had she tried recipes on until she found one that worked? How many people had died in the process?

I opened my eyes and Cole was watching me with an intensity that bordered on dangerous. He brushed his fingertips across my eyes. "I see what they mean by Valentine resolution."

I gave a half smile. "Cole, you've told me a hundred times that I have the ability to command this family, to make them follow orders I set."

"Second only to your father although he doesn't concern himself much with the business side of things any longer."

"And you."

"Actually, you can overrule me, Ariana. Were we to disagree, the men would follow your orders rather than mine. Even if it were the wrong decision and got them killed, they would follow you."

"It's not my intention to get anyone killed."

"No, but it could happen. You are new to this world and may not recognize a lot of the dangers that exist. I consider it part of my job to make sure you are aware of those things. So, I suggest that you and I make sure we're always in agreement where family business is concerned. Clearly, you've made some resolution in your head so let's see if we can come to a compromise."

"So you assume we're going to disagree?"

"There is no doubt in my mind."

I laughed. "How many people know the recipe for my mother's drug? The one she gave me."

"Ah," Cole frowned and shook his head. "Yes, we are definitely going to disagree. It will be a battle with your father as well, though for entirely different reasons. Four, as of right now."

He obviously knew what I was going to say, but I was determined to make it clear anyway. "I don't want the house of Valentine to manufacture it. Ever."

"We'll start with your father's objections. It will be damn profitable."

"That's it? That will be his only reasoning?"

Cole considered. "He might try the emotional avenue...it was Teresa's last and most notable creation. Her life's work, so to speak."

"Tony's new concoction is worth a million times more than her recipe. It's a legitimate market which means safer and less hassle. With both drugs already having FDA approval, there is no lag time. It could go into the market tomorrow. Switch up the components in different percentages and you'll have a damn addictive street drug as well. Whichever method appeals."

"Or both. Both will appeal to the Valentine bottom line." Cole nodded his approval.

"My mother was many more things some drug. That is not what she deserves to be known for."

"True, but not convincing enough to dissuade Franco."

I sighed. "Her most notable creation was the one she made with my father...me. I was her life's work, and the drug was merely a way to keep me safe until my father, the only true love of her life, could be at my side once again."

"Absolutely true," he gave me a quick kiss, "and fucking cunning as hell. You almost had *me* ready to give in."

"But?"

"But," he ran a finger down my cheek, "until we find a way to safely wean you from it, without the drug you'll die."

"I don't think it would-"

"Ariana, you've no idea how close I came to losing you so please don't belittle it. This is our job; it's what we do. A half hour longer and you would have dropped into circulatory shock, and you would never have awoken. If Tony hadn't figured it out, if you had been too far gone to identify the substance, if I hadn't known where to get the missing component, you would be dead. We were lucky, and I'm not willing to leave your life up to chance."

"So...stalemate."

"No," he chuckled. "Compromise. We will continue to manufacture it but only for your use. It's just an addition to Valentine so Tony can do that himself. But, once we find a way to get you off it, we'll never make it again. Assuming you get your father to agree."

"Compromise didn't work so well for my parents."

"We are not them, Ariana. Despite what history you think is repeating itself, we can choose the path we take."

"As long as it's together, I don't give a damn about anything else."

"You can be romantic," he chuckled, nuzzling my neck. He gave me a long, drawn kiss before pulling a breath away. "You and I, Ariana, will make the world jealous."